SNATCHED UP BY A DON

A BBW LOVE STORY

P. WISE

CONTENTS

STAY CONNECTED

Instagram: @CEO.Pwise

Facebook: Author P. Wise

Facebook Business: Authoress P. Wise

Facebook Group: Words of the Wise (P. Wise Book Group)

CHAPTER 1

LYRIC LARSON

R*ing! Ring! Ring!*
My husband, Chadd's, phone rang out and went to voicemail for the fourth time. Looking at the time in the top left corner of my iPhone, it read ten twenty-three p.m. He should've been home a long time ago, but I knew the position he held at the investment firm sometimes had him pulling late hours. There were even times he would lock himself in his office in the house until the wee hours in the morning working.

Another lonely night, I thought.

I powered off my laptop and closed it. My writing goal of five thousand words was completed for the day, so I felt accomplished. Being a full-time author was very demanding.

Some people thought it was just to write a book and get it published. Little did they know, it took so much work and it could be mentally draining, especially if other things distracted you from getting the work done. For instance, when Chadd went MIA and I wouldn't hear from him, it bothered my soul and I started to think all kinds of things, causing me to not be able to focus on writing.

Just when I was about to plug my phone up to the charger and head in the shower, it chimed with my best friend, Nick's, name appearing on the screen

Nicky Pooh: I know you got those words in, so go get you some dick and get some rest. Goodnight, love you, muah!

Me: Mmmhmmm, right. Goodnight, baby, I love you more!

If only you knew. I rolled my eyes.

Nick was my everything. If he wasn't gay, he'd probably been my husband. We met in high school, sophomore year. He transferred mid-school year and, of course, with his feminine and flamboyant ways, it was hard for him to fit in. Me not being the friendly welcome committee, I didn't approach him. But, on his first day, he asked for directions, and we had on the same latest Jordan's that released. We made small conversation and it turned into us hanging out. Years later, we were closer than conjoining twins.

Finally plugging my phone and laptop up to the chargers, I undressed myself and headed into the bathroom. I jumped in the shower and washed my skin, making sure to get every crease and curve. Once I was satisfied with how well I took care of my hygiene, I stepped out the shower and dried my skin.

As I went back into the bedroom and was searching through my night clothes drawer for something to put on to sleep, I saw a bunch of my lingerie and an idea came to mind. Instead of putting on pajamas, I slide myself into a nice neon pink lingerie. I wanted to surprise Chadd since I knew he had a long day, and it had been a while since we were intimate.

Just when I finished getting dressed, I heard the house alarm and the code being punched in to reset, letting me know he had reached home. I quickly sprayed some Victoria's Secret body spray on my body to smell even better, cut the light out and laid on the bed to wait for him.

Moments later, he walked in the room and turned the lights on with a shocked face.

"What the hell is this?" he quizzed with a confused look on his face.

"I thought I'd surprise you since—"

He bussed out laughing while I was mid-sentence, cutting me completely off.

"Lyric, what in the fuck are you wearing?" he blurted out. "You look like a huge glow-in-the-dark pink teddy bear. Now, why would you ever think that shit was sexy?" He continued to laugh hysterically.

If I had just an inch of confidence, it was out the window once Chadd opened his mouth and violated. Too embarrassed to throw a comeback his way, I rolled out the bed and rushed into the bathroom. I sat on the toilet and cried silent cries, asking God why was I the way I was and why was Chadd not in love with me anymore.

I couped myself up in the bathroom for a while before I finally snapped out of it. I decided to take a nice hot bath to relax my mind and my nerves. Even though I took a shower already, I just needed to wash away the negative feeling I felt and clear my mind; a bath always helped me with that.

I ran the hot water, dropped in a Sweet To Me bath bomb by Keyology, lit my strawberry scented candle from Au'Shay Home, and turned on my meditation playlist on my iPad.

Before I stepped into the tub, I looked in the mirror and observed my body as I always did. The same thoughts plagued my mind; my old self was a distant memory. I was now just downright fat and ugly. I used to be the slim, thick chick that attracted everyone from the way my hips swayed. But once my health changed and I started to gain massive weight, I got no attention at all, not even from my husband.

My doctor diagnosed me with PCOS, Polycystic Ovaries Syndrome, which came with so many different symptoms. I was bleeding for months, unable to have sex, my weight peeked uncontrollably, and there were major problems in the fertility department. All this caused me to go into a deep depression where I ate for comfort. I was no longer the same woman my husband married, and I couldn't give him a child, no matter how many times we tried. I was useless.

Shaking off the thoughts of how I got to the size I was, I took my time and climbed into the tub. Easing my body down into the bubble-filled water, I rested my head back on my tub pillow and relaxed.

Subconsciously, my hand slid down between my legs and met my pearl of pleasure. I ran my fingers past it a few times before I eventually started to massage it. I felt my body getting warm, and it wasn't because of the water. I continued to play with my clit as I imagined Chadd being between my legs licking me dry like he used to. Moving my hips in a circle, I applied pressure to my clit and, just when I was about to slip a finger in my pussy, I sensed someone's presence, so I opened my eyes.

"Don't stop because I'm here. Do your thing," Chadd said with amusement in his voice and a grin on his face.

I rolled my eyes and closed them back again. "I wouldn't have to do it if my husband did what he had to do," I retorted sarcastically.

Chadd hadn't touched me in months, even after the bleeding stopped. He refused to show me any kind of affection. Time and time again, I expressed my feelings, but nothing changed.

"Here we go. I don't have time for that tonight; I just had the longest day ever." He waved me off and walked out the bathroom.

I reached out the tub and turned up the volume on the speakers. I didn't want to hear anything he was doing in the bedroom. I needed the music to take me to another world, so my mind wasn't on him or of my unhappy life.

Another thirty minutes or so passed, and I finally climbed out the tub. I dried off, applied lotion to my skin, and got dressed, all in the bathroom. I was very self-conscious of myself and didn't like to change in front on Chadd. There were times I caught him cringing at the sight of me. Once it happened on a few occasions, I made a mental note and never got dressed around him anymore.

When I walked into our bedroom, Chadd wasn't there, so I walked about the house to find him. Of course, he was in his office. As I approached the closed door, I could hear him having a low tone conversation with someone.

"Believe me, I'm not happy with this situation and I'm trying my best to get out of it as soon as possible," I heard him tell the person on the other end of the phone.

It got silent for a few moments, so I assumed he was listening to what they had to say. Not wanting to stand there any longer, I knocked on the door and walked into his office.

"Hey, what are you doing?" I asked.

With a stunned facial expression, he quickly removed the phone from his ear and hung up. "Oh, nothing just speaking to John about an account; it's been stressing us out. You good?" He tried to brush things off and change the subject.

I hated confrontation, especially when we just had a slight one, so I left it alone, even though I was far from stupid. I also didn't have solid proof of anything, so it wasn't a good idea to come right out and accuse him of anything.

"I'm alright. My brain is shot from today's writing, had a tough one, so I'm about to go get some rest." I played it off, not showing my suspicion.

"Cool, hopefully, I can get to bed soon, just have to finish up some stuff." He shot me a weak smile.

"Okay, goodnight."

I turned on my heels and exited out his office with a more

uncertain feeling than I did when I first entered. Chadd used to be the man I couldn't keep my eyes off. He was tall and handsome with blue eyes. Although he was Caucasian, he had a swagger on him that not many of his kind could pull off.

We met during our college years at NYU, where he studied finance and I studied literature. We were on total opposite paths careerwise, as well as our social crowds but, somehow, God made us meet. Sometimes, I wondered why he made us cross paths.

When I got back into our bedroom, I checked my phone and laptop once more before getting in bed. I saw there weren't any notifications, so I crawled my ass in between the sheets and comforter and went to sleep, hoping my dreams would make me happy because reality wasn't doing it.

THE FOLLOWING MORNING, I woke up to an empty side of the bed. It wasn't even slept in, which only told me Chadd fell asleep in his office or went into one of the guest rooms we had. That was something he would do when we had an argument or claimed to not want to be bothered due to stress from work.

I thanked God for waking me up. Instead of my usual routine of checking my phone and emails, I rolled out of bed and went looking for Chadd. Searching all the guest rooms, I came up empty, so with only two last places to look: the living room and his office. I proceeded downstairs to look.

Passing through the living area, I saw no sign of him. I went to his office but, before I even made it anywhere near the door, I saw it was open. Walking inside, I noticed the place was empty.

Where the hell are you?

Immediately, I went to the front of the house to see if his car was in the driveway. As I looked out the window, Chadd's car was slowing pulling in. I didn't move an inch. I watched, as he opened the driver door and stepped out in gym attire with his gym bag in his hands.

I sighed in relief; there I was thinking the worst when all he did was hit the gym, probably to release some stress. Giggling to myself, I quickly ran to the kitchen, so he wouldn't have saw I was watching him from the window. Preparing to make some coffee, I heard the front door open and shut.

"Baby? Is that you?" I asked before he came into plain sight. "Good morning, where were you?" I asked, even though it was obvious.

"I couldn't sleep, so I decided to hit the gym. I'm taking today off anyway. I need some rest," he answered. "Good morning, by the way." He came and kissed me on the cheek, then left out the kitchen.

Keeping up the act, I continued to make the coffee, and drank some of it before heading back upstairs to get ready to start my day. When I reached back into the room, he was removing his clothes to get in the shower, something I was getting ready to do. To not make a fuss, I just grabbed my towel and things and went into one of the guest bathrooms.

As I washed up, my mind drifted off to what my day was going to consist of. I had a meeting about my upcoming book release. Then, I had a lunch date with Nick and my sister, Lori-Ann and, of course, returning home to write.

Thinking about my schedule, that's when it hit me that my car was still in the shop from the previous day and wouldn't be ready until the next day or so.

Shit, I hate traveling and taking Ubers.

Finishing up in the shower, I got out and got myself together. Once dressed, I went back into our bedroom that we somewhat shared and found him lying on the bed, scrolling through his phone.

"Hey, my car is still in the shop. Since you're staying in today, do you mind if I use your car? I'll be back by three." I clasped my hands together in a begging position. "I just have my launch meeting and then lunch with Nick and Lori-Ann."

"That's cool, go ahead," he simply responded.

I walked to the side of the bed he laid on, bent down and gave him a peek on his lips. He quickly moved away, stretched, and got comfortable under the comforter. I brushed it off as him being tired because he usually didn't have a problem kissing me, it was the least he could've done since he wasn't giving me none.

Gathering my things I needed for the day, I headed down-stairs, grabbed the car keys off the key hook by the door and left out the house. When I got in the car, I smelled a sweet smell, which raised an alarm in my head and had my mind wandering. I mashed down on the brake and pressed the start button to get the car warmed back up on that cold winter morning.

As I was pulling out of the driveway and onto the street, a call came in but, instead of a name being saved, it was the water splash emoji. *Who the fuck is this?*

I didn't even get a chance to do anything. The call was answered, which told me Chadd's phone was still connected to the car's Bluetooth.

"Baby, I miss you already, come back," the girl cooed throughout the car speakers.

The voice sounded so familiar; I froze for a minute, trying to recognize it.

"Hello? Hello? Chadd?" she called out.

That's when the call was disconnected from the car due to the distance from his phone. Instead of turning the car around and running back inside to confront Chadd, I continued to drive while trying to match a face with the voice and, finally doing so, I tried talking myself out of thinking the way I was.

She wouldn't, I thought.

CHADD LARSON

"Hellooo!" yelled Kayla.

"Hello?" I answered for damn near the tenth time.

"Oh, there you are. I been talking and didn't hear you," she explained.

"I didn't hear you at all. My phone was still connected to my car," I concluded.

Ahh shit, I had just realized what I said.

Lyric left with my car and, if it was still connected to it, she had to have heard Kayla when she answered the phone, unless she didn't. Lyric was a very vocal person and didn't hide her feelings or if she had to get something off her chest so, if she'd heard Kayla, I was pretty sure she'd come back in the house and raise hell. Since she didn't confront me, she couldn't have heard it, so I told myself I was in the clear, but I'd still watch how she moved.

"Oh okay, well, I'm missing the hell out of you. It almost felt like I was about to wake up to you this morning but, instead, you were already gone," she whined.

"Kayla, stop," I shut her down.

Kayla was my assistant of two years who I grew to like, then eventually love. What's crazy was Kayla was only hired by me because of Lyric. They met when Lyric went to a restaurant and saw how Kayla was being mistreated by the other staff members. She took her number and later advocated for her to get a job with me.

Trusting my wife's opinion, I hired her, and Lyric was right. Kayla was a very hard worker and did as she was told; I never had any problems with her. The only thing I didn't see was me falling for her while married to Lyric.

"I'm sorry, but you know how I feel," she pleaded.

"I know. Matter of fact, what are you doing right now?"

"Nothing, you called out, so I got off today as well," she reminded me.

"Come over. Lyric is gone until late in the afternoon," I informed her as I looked at my phone for a quick second to see the time, which read eight forty-nine a.m.

"Chadd, what? You're playing around, right?"

"No, I'm serious, come. She has a long meeting this morning and then having lunch with her best friend and sister."

"I mean, if you think we won't get caught, then fine. I'll come right now."

"Why you still on the phone then?"

"Call you when I'm leaving out," she squealed and hung up right after.

I remained in bed as I waited for Kayla's arrival and, while doing so, my mind ran on Lyric and how we were in the beginning.

Lyric and I had been married for two and a half years, a little before Kayla and I were introduced, but we were in a relationship for about seven years prior to getting married, so we were together for a good ten years. Our entire relationship, we agreed that having kids wasn't smart until we were married, living together, and deep into our careers, so we waited. Lyric and I traveled the world, experienced different things together and enjoyed each other.

When I felt it was the right time to pop the question, I did. Since then, I had not been able to get a child from her and we're both thirty years old. My parents kept reminding me that we weren't getting any younger and that the older a woman got, the harder it was for them to conceive.

While we battled with the whole fertility situation, Lyric started to lose herself. She wasn't the same woman I met in college or even married. Lyric was beautiful. When she walked into a room, she demanded your attention. Her gorgeous, light-brown skin tone was always blemish free. She had hypnotizing light brown eyes with full lips. Her body was something out of a magazine: nice size waist with hips and ass for days.

My friends used to joke on me and asked how I was handling all of that but, since she gained so much weight just over a year, they really joked and ask me that. While I would laugh and crack jokes back, deep down, I felt embarrassed.

The doctor told her she had something called PCOS, which caused her to gain weight, along with other crazy symptoms. At a point, we weren't even sexually active because she was bleeding for months straight. I tried to convince her to give me head or even let me fuck her in the ass, but she just wouldn't budge. She claimed she had no desire for sexual acts; the bleeding and depression was taking over. Since she didn't care about my needs, I went outside and got it handled, which happened to be by Kayla. I loved Lyric, with everything in me, but I was slowly falling out of love with her and in love with Kayla.

My phone rang, immediately pulling me from my thoughts. "Hello?"

"I just left out. I'm in an Uber coming now," Kayla informed me.

"Okay, call me when you're near."

Finally getting out the bed, I ran downstairs and made a cup of coffee from what Lyric had made a little earlier. I went into my office and checked any emails that may have come in and was quick to respond to, otherwise, I wasn't replying back to anyone or bussing my brain for the next person. I just wanted a day to relax my mind and not think about work or needy ass clients.

By the time I was finished browsing through emails, Kayla was calling me again.

"You near?"

"Yeah, I'm literally one minute away," she notified.

"Okay, when you get here, make sure you look around the area before getting out and walking up to the door," I instructed.

We had some very nosy neighbors, and they wouldn't mind telling Lyric that they saw a female coming into our home when she wasn't here.

"No one's out here," Kayla stated.

I walked to the front of the house and looked out the window to see the car slowly driving up to the house. "Alright, come on," I told her quickly.

After the line went dead, seconds later, the car came to a complete stop and she busted through the back door, swiftly making her way to the front door. I opened the door right as she reached it, and she ran inside right into my arms. I closed the door back as soon as her foot was in the clear.

"Hi, baby," Kayla sang as she held onto me tight.

I kissed her on her forehead and guided her towards the steps to go upstairs.

Kayla was as stunning as they came. She was tall and slim with a little booty and cute, small perky breasts, and her complexion was of a caramel tone. She had cat eyes, with round shaped lips and long hair to complement her look.

"Your house is beautiful, Chadd," Kayla spoke as she looked around.

She'd never been upstairs before, only downstairs and out back when Lyric and I held a few events and invited some coworkers over. "Thanks, Lyric did everything, that's more her thing," I blurted out.

"Oh, I see," she responded in a low tone.

I wrapped my hands around her waist from behind and hugged her tightly. Her small frame would always fit perfectly in my arms. She wiggled out of my embrace, dropped to her knees, and pulled down my basketball shorts. Exposing my semi-hard penis, she toyed with it for a few seconds, then placed it in her mouth.

"Ohhh," I groaned out loud.

We were at the foot of my bed and, by the time I was all the way hard, she was already making my knees weak. I plumped down on the bed, making her stop for a split second, but then returned to what she was doing immediately after my ass touched the sheets. I grabbed a handful of her hair and guided her up and down my tool. Her little round lips meant nothing; she knew how to deep throat better than any woman I'd ever had.

After a good while of Kayla blessing me with her talents, she came up for air and started to strip out of her clothes. Before she climbed on top of me, she stopped and looked around.

"You sure you want to do this on the bed you share with Lyric?" she asked with sincerity in her voice.

She was right, and I was glad she stopped to ask because I was in such a mood that I didn't notice what I was doing. Yes, things were rocky between Lyric and me, but she didn't deserve any of what I was doing to her, and to have another woman in the bed she laid her head would've been the ultimate disrespect.

"Let's go in one of the guest rooms," I advised.

We left out the master bedroom and entered into the closest guest room. Not wasting another second, we climbed in bed and attacked each other.

I fucked Kayla within every each of that room with no regards to if I even destroyed a lamp or made a picture fall off the wall and break. In that moment, making love to her was my only concern; I'd deal with Lyric later.

LYRIC

"Okay, so the party will start at six o'clock, but the signing will begin at approximately eight o'clock," I heard one of the young ladies on my marketing team announce.

My mind was so far gone, I was barely able to concentrate on my book release meeting. They were speaking, and all I heard were muffled tones with clear words here and there. I tried my best to keep a straight face and not allow anyone to see my true mood because at the end of the day, it was business and they were there to do a job, not have any concern about my personal issues.

"What do you think about everything?" one of the ladies asked.

"It sounds great. I trust you all to make sure the night turns out successful. You've done it before, so I know you'll do it again," I expressed.

My publisher eyed me out the corner of her eyes, but I didn't pay her any mind. Once I was finished speaking, she spoke up and started telling them about additional things she wanted to fit in within the night. That's when I slowly drifted back off into my own little world.

About a half an hour later, the meeting was finally over. Everyone cleared out the conference room except for my publisher, Irene, and myself. I just sat there staring into space, motionless.

"Lyric!" Irene shouted, immediately grabbing my attention.

I jumped and looked over at her standing there with her hands on her hips. "I'm sorry, Irene," I simply said.

"What's going on sugar, you alright?" She walked over to me and rubbed my back.

Irene was an older woman who was not only my publisher but someone like an aunt. I'd been signed to her publishing house since I came out of college, and I'd had so much success being under her. Besides business, she'd helped me through a lot of tough times in my life, so she was more than just a boss to me.

"No, I'm not, honestly." I lowered my head.

"You feel like you want to talk about it?"

"Not just yet because I'm not a hundred percent sure of what's going on," I voiced.

"I understand. Well, whenever you're ready, I'm here

baby." She kissed me on my head and walked out the conference room, leaving me to drown in my thoughts.

———————

AFTER SITTING in the meeting room for what felt like forever, I finally got myself up and left. I jumped in the car and texted both Nick and Lori-Ann to let them know I was on my way to the restaurant we were meeting at. They both responded almost immediately, letting me know they were heading there too.

While I made my way through the Manhattan streets, I tried my best to dodge the traffic but, if you're from New York, you know that's inevitable. My mind kept tugging back and forth with me about if I should go meet Nick and Lori-Ann or if I should just head back home to Staten Island.

I knew deep down it wouldn't end well if I went home, and my mind was all over the place. Nick and Lori-Ann was the perfect people to sit down with and get everything off my chest; they were also great at advice and didn't choose sides. They had no problem letting me know when I was wrong or overthinking the situation.

Passing the restaurant, I drove a few feet away and pulled into the parking lot they had. As if it was perfect timing, I saw both Nick and Lori-Ann exiting their vehicles with big smiles on their faces. Seeing them made my mood shift a bit. They had that aura about them that wouldn't allow you to be in a miserable mood, especially with Nick being the life of the party all the time.

SNATCHED UP BY A DON

"Lyric! Lori!" Nike sang, as we all approached each other.

"Hi, my babies," Lori greeted us.

"Heyyy, y'all," I sang.

We all took turns hugging and kissing each other. When we were done, we headed inside the restaurant where the hostess sat us right away since we made reservations. As we place our orders for drinks and food, the conversations started without a second being wasted.

"So, how's everyone doing?" Nick asked with a big smile on his face.

It had been close to a month we hadn't met in that manner. Lori was a stay-at-home mom with four children, and Nick was a traveling fashion stylist who was in high demand and, well me, I had to get my books completed so I was always home behind the computer screen.

"Same ol, I'm mommied out, man. I need a vacation and I don't want to see my kids for like two weeks," Lori whined.

"Sheesh, thanks for letting me know motherhood ain't all that great," I teased, making us all laugh.

"It's an amazing thing, but it can also get overwhelming when you're the only person that's tending to four children all day, every day," she expressed.

"Yeah, that sounds draining, love," Nick stated, scrunching up his face.

"Nick!" I raised my voice.

He shrugged and waved me off.

"No, he's right, Lyric, it is. Take your time and enjoy your life before pushing one out," she advised.

Little do you know, I want one now, I said to myself.

I nodded my head in acknowledgment. "Mr. Hot Shot Nick," I sang. "How's the fashion world treating you my dear?"

He flipped his imaginary hair and sat up in his seat.

"It's treating me well, my love," he sang with a smile on his face.

"I'm so happy for you, friend. Look at you, living your dream," I beamed at him.

Nick came a long way and, despite all the trials and tribulations that tried to get in his way, he didn't allow it to take him down. He pushed on and made something of himself and didn't care what anyone had to say; he believed in himself.

"Thanks, baby. What's going on with you? You seem okay, but I can tell when you're trying to mask something." He raised his eyebrows.

"Yeah, something feels off about you," Lori added.

I looked at the two of them and took a deep breath. "Chadd's cheating on me," I blurted out quickly.

They sat there and starred at me, allowing silence to take over. I hung my head because I knew that would've been their reaction. Once before, I accused Chadd of cheating but didn't have any proof. I just went off of how he was acting but, come to find out, he wasn't having an affair, so I was left feeling and looking stupid. This time around was different though; I heard it with my own two ears.

"It's for real this time. I heard it myself," I went on.

"How so?" Nick asked, resting his arm on the table and placing his chin in his palm.

"Well, you both saw I came here with his car. Mine is in the shop. When I was driving away from the house, a call came in and it connected to the car. The girl said she missed him already and called him baby," I explained. "He came in right after I woke up, claiming to come from the gym but, obviously, after I heard the phone call, I knew he was with someone."

"Wow, you can't be serious, Lyric," Nick said in a low tone with a surprised expression.

"And you won't believe who I think it is." I looked at both of them.

"Who?" Lori asked with urgency.

"Kayla."

"Get the fuck out of here," Nick snapped.

Lori held her hands to her mouth in disbelief.

"I know her voice all too well, but I want to be sure before I approach either of them."

"I strongly suggest you do that, friend. This is a major accusation and, although I believe you, you have to have proof for others if you decide to leave or even tell anyone else outside our circle," Nick voiced.

"You're right, so that's what I'll do. Play it cool and collect evidence," I stated.

Evidence was definitely needed if I wanted to file a divorce. Leaving on my own, I would leave our marriage with nothing but, if he was guilty of any infidelity, I would get almost everything, and that's something he would hate to happen.

Our meals came, so we ate and started speaking about

other things. For some reason, letting them know what I found out was like a weight lifted off my shoulders, even though I didn't confront Chadd or Kayla.

With my mood lightened, we enjoyed our lunch and continued to play catch up. It was definitely something I needed. When it was all said and done, I had to face my reality and head back home to pretend everything was normal, or at least as normal as could be with Chadd and me.

I hugged my best friend and sister goodbye, hopped in the car, and headed towards the Verrazano Bridge to get to Staten Island.

Lord, please keep me calm, I prayed.

Two hours and a ton of traffic later, I was finally pulling into our driveway. As I stepped out of the car, Mrs. Lawrence from across the street came out her front door and waved me over.

Lord, what this old woman want now?

Mrs. Lawrence was one of the few elders in the neighborhood, our block particularly, who liked to be nosy and in other people's business, so I hesitated to even go across the street. Against my better judgement, I went anyway.

"Hi, Mrs. Lawrence, how are you today?" I asked as I approached her.

"I'm fine, honey. How are you is the question," she shot back.

"I'm doing well, can't complain," I simply said.

"I have something to show you. Come inside for a quick minute." She turned around and motioned for me to follow her, so I did.

When we got inside, she went to a table that was in the hallway and picked up a small device that had a screen on it. When I looked closely, it was a camera surveillance monitor.

She clicked a few buttons on the screen and a playback came on. It was an unfamiliar car slowly pulling up to my house and, moments later, Kayla emerged from the backseat and rushed her way into my house.

This mother fucker and this hoe ass bitch.

"Mrs. Lawrence, is there any way you can get that to my email by chance?" I politely asked her.

"I don't know how to, but I can ask my grandson to do it when he gets in later," she informed me.

"I would greatly appreciate that," I said, trying to keep my composure. "Here's my email address." I wrote it down on a piece of paper I had in my bag and handed it to her.

"Okay, I will give this to him as soon as he gets in," she assured me.

"Thank you so much, Mrs. Lawrence," I emphasized as I made my way out her front door.

I walked across the street with so much hurt, pain, and anger building up inside me. I didn't think it was a wise decision for me to go into the house at that moment. I unlocked the car and hopped in. Starting it back up, I pulled out the driveway and pressed the gas in the direction opposite of my home.

While I wanted to beat the shit out of Kayla, the main

31

person I was disappointed in and torn apart by was my husband. How could he have done something like that to me? It was one thing to cheat, but to bring your mistress into my home where I laid my head and claimed safe heaven was a whole other ball game.

I drove around to collect my thoughts and relax my nerves. Something had to be done, but I had to go about things a smart way. I promised myself I was going to get the last laugh when everything was over, and I planned on keeping that promise.

CHADD

The way Kayla and I were having sex around the house, you would've thought it was our first time, but it wasn't. I'd been dealing with her for a good year, but the recent few months was when we started to get more serious.

While enjoying Kayla's company, I kept checking my phone and windows every other minute to make sure Lyric didn't come back early. I made sure to have Kayla stuff in one place in case she did; I could've gotten her out the back in a hurry. Thankfully, Lyric came back just about the time she said she would, and I had Kayla long gone about two hours before.

I cleaned up the house, well, the places we frequented,

changed the sheets in the guest room, and made sure there were no traces of another woman. Once I was finished with all of the straightening up, I relaxed, and an idea came to mind. I decided it was time to take Lyric out on a date.

My mood and mind was in a good space. Lyric was getting ready to release yet another novel, so it was a perfect celebratory dinner idea for just the two of us. Plus, I knew she'd love the thought since she was always nagging me about not doing things with her and showing her enough attention and affection. I needed to keep her off my back and not suspicious anyway, until I knew what I wanted to do.

Lyric returned back home around three thirty, just like she said she would. I was in my office when she came in and decided to stay there until I knew how she was feeling exactly. I wanted to be sure she didn't hear Kayla on the Bluetooth and, the way Lyric was, it was hard for her to conceal her true emotions, so she was never the kind of person to try to hide it.

"Baby?" I heard her yell out once she closed the house door.

"Yeah, I'm in my office!" I shouted back.

Moments later, she appeared by the entrance of my office. "Hey, I thought you were taking a day's break from work?" she asked as she leaned up against the doorframe.

"I am, just looking at something small. How was the meeting and lunch?" I leaned back, awaiting her response.

"Meeting was annoying; everyone had different ideas and couldn't come to an agreement. We're meeting again later this week," she rolled her eyes as she explained. "But, on another note, lunch with Nick and Lori-Ann was great. I needed that, felt like I haven't been out in forever," she went on to express.

"Speaking of out, we're going to dinner tonight, so go pick out something nice to wear," I announced.

Her face was shocked as she jumped back and held her chest. "Are you serious, Mr. Larson?" she asked sarcastically, placing her hand on her hip.

"I'm serious, Mrs. Larson," I chuckled.

"Alright then, let me go see what I'm wearing." She turned around and walked off.

That didn't go too bad. She definitely didn't hear anything, I thought.

I returned my attention to what I was doing on the computer for a little while longer; then, I shut down everything and headed upstairs to see what I was going to wear to dinner myself.

For the next few hours, we just lounged around the house and did our own thing until it was time to get ready. Being as though we both decided to get in the shower at the same time, something we did often, I volunteered to go into one of the guest rooms to do so.

As I was walking in the room, Lyric was passing by. She looked my way. Her eyes landed inside the room and stopped.

"Are those new sheets?" she asked as she pointed at the bedding.

"Ahhh, yeah. When I was going to look out the window, clumsy me tripped and spilled soda on the comforter, so I just took everything off and put on a new fresh set," I quickly blurted out. I didn't think she'd notice that the bedding was changed, so I had to find a lie off the back to say.

"Oh, okay," she simply said and walked off.

I let out a deep breath. I caught myself holding in once she was out of eye and ear shot.

We got ourselves ready for dinner and, within a good hour and a half, we were walking out the door and getting in the car to go to the restaurant. Since the night was dedicated to her and her hard work, I decided to take her to one of her favorite spots in the city.

"Awwwh, baby, you must really be in a good ass mood," she cooed, as I pulled up front of the place.

"You deserve it." I shot her a wink and got out the car to rush to her side to open her door.

Grabbing ahold of my hand, she climbed out the car and stepped beside me. The valet handed me a card, and we proceeded inside where the hostess greeted us.

"Reservations for the Larsons, please," I told the woman at the hostess stand.

She took a second to look at her chart, looked up and smiled at us but, I before she did that, she gave Lyric a funny look and looked at me with lustful eyes.

"Right this way, Mr. Larson," she stated and motioned for us to follow her.

I prayed Lyric didn't pay her any attention and caught up to the way she was acting.

Many women, Caucasian at that, would turn their nose up when they saw Lyric and I out together, especially once they found out we were married. They would give her nasty looks as if she wasn't worthy of being with me, and it only got worse when she gained the weight. It wasn't just my friends I had to deal with, it was also strangers.

"Your waitress will be right with you," the woman said before walking off.

She walked in the direction Lyric was sitting so, as a man, I couldn't help not notice her nicely figured body, but I quickly reverted my attention back to my wife. I didn't even like white girls, I never had.

"Women just won't stop gawking at you; it always been this way since college," Lyric joked.

She had a sense of humor when it came to women since she knew she was the one with the ring and was leaving to go home with me. There were barely instances where Lyric ever got jealous. She didn't allow women to see her sweat even if she felt a way, which was rare.

The waitress finally came, greeted us, and took our orders. The wait overall wasn't long, and the food was remarkable as always. Lyric and I talked, laughed, and caught up on things we didn't notice we hadn't told each other about our careers. It was a night out that was much needed; I believe we both appreciated each other's company.

When we got back home, the party didn't end. Changing out our clothes, we decided to pour another glass of wine, kick back and chill. Few glasses later, we were feeling it and ended up making out but, as soon as we started to get further, I abruptly stopped.

"What's wrong?" she asked with a confused expression.

"I'm tired and should get in bed, have an early start in the morning." I stood to my feet and grabbed both of our wine glasses to take to the kitchen.

"But we were..." her voice trailed off as she hung her head.

I walked back in the living room and lifted her chin with my index finger so that we were face to face. "Another night, I love you." I kissed her lips before leaving out the living area and heading upstairs.

While I was horny, I remembered I had just sexed Kayla a million times earlier that day, and my guilty conscious started to mess with me. I just hoped she got over it, and I made a mental note to try to make it up to her.

———

THE NEXT MORNING, I was up before the sun even decided to rise. I had a mind that taking a day off randomly was going to come back and bite me in the ass, so I had to mentally prepare myself for the day I was going to have. Lyric was still asleep, so I moved about the house quietly to get ready. From the time I woke up, I started working from home but quickly got myself together to get to the office since most of the things I needed was there. Within a good hour, I was out the door and head into the place that paid me well but stressed my soul.

The sun was now rising as I made my way down the highway to get onto the bridge. I liked to get a head start over others because the traffic going into the city could get unbearable in the morning, and I hated public transportation.

Beating the New York morning rush, I pulled into the parking garage of the office a little before six o'clock a.m. I parked in my spot, grabbed my briefcase and phone, then headed to the building's entrance. As I was opening the door to walk inside to the elevator, a huge hand grabbed ahold of my shoulders and pushed me against the wall.

"Mr. Luchiano would like a word," the tall husky man said in an Italian accent.

I turned around to see two black tinted Escalades parked up not far from the entrance with another guy standing outside the driver side of the vehicle. I nodded my head, as he guided me to the truck as if I had any other choice.

Climbing in the backseat of the truck, Mr. Luchiano sat there patiently, facing forward. Don Luchiano was a very feared and wealthy mob boss; he was the head of the Luchiano Mafia that spread across the United States and Italy. He came to me in my beginning years of being an investor and offered me a ton of money to make sure he went unseen.

"How is business?" he asked, referring to his money trail.

"It's great, no complaints," I responded immediately.

"Mmm, good. How's your wife, what's her name, Lyric?" He turned his face towards me a little.

"Uh, yes, sir. Lyric, she's doing well, thanks for asking."

The door to my side of the vehicle swung open, and I saw a black guy standing there; his features were similar to Don Luchiano.

"This is my son, Logan; you will be seeing him more often. I'm heading out the country for a short travel.

Anything comes up, contact him." He pointed towards his son, as Logan handed me his card with his information on it.

I nodded my head up and down in acknowledgment and took the card from him. Logan stepped to the side and motioned his hand for me to exit the truck. Once I stepped my foot out, he got in, along with their bodyguards and both Escalades peeled out of the parking garage, leaving me standing there shook.

Being in their presence always made my body shake in fear. The Luchi's weren't a friendly kind of organization. You had to watch how you spoke and answered them, and it was vital you listened to their orders carefully.

My feet felt like they were cemented to the ground, unable to move for about a good five minutes. If a car driving in and trying to park in the spot I stood in didn't blow their horn, I probably would've still been stuck in the same place.

I swiftly walked to the elevator and headed upstairs to my office. Once inside, I shut the door, sat down, and took a couple deep breaths to calm my nerves. They say another man should never put fear in your heart but, in my case, anyone who had the Luchiano blood running through their veins had me scared for my life. One wrong move and that could be my last move.

LOGAN "LO" LUCHIANO

"**W**atch him closely. I have the accountants auditing everything from the moment I hired him," my pops stated as soon as we pulled out the parking garage.

"Bet." I nodded.

If my father was having thorough checks done on his money, that meant he saw something that wasn't right or his gut was telling him something. He was a man of honor so, before he accused anyone of anything, he always liked to have solid proof to bring to them. From there, he would either allow them to explain and, depending on the severity of everything, he would make his decision on how he wanted to discipline the person. This went for everyone, including family.

We rode back to his house in Staten Island in silence. It was early in the morning when people started to make their way to work or to drop their kids off to school. We drove all the way to Manhattan just to see one of his cleaners, Chadd. Chadd was hired by my father some time ago, and I'd always heard about him but never met him until that morning.

I had to work my way up the ranks within the family organization and, yet, I was still low, all because I was not full-blown Italian; I was a nigga. My father had an affair with my mother while he was married to his wife. Because they had problems conceiving, my father didn't allow my mother to abort me. He didn't know if that was his only chance at having a child, so he went against the tradition of an Italian family and had a child with an African American woman.

My pops, Don Lorenzo Luchiano, wasn't your typical mobster. He didn't have a million mistresses that he had to keep up with. My mother caught his eyes when they were younger, and he eventually fell in love with her. His marriage at the time was an arrangement and had no true feelings, plus, he couldn't get a child out of her, so it was a difficult situation for him. My mother was his escape and, in the process of them falling for each other, I was created.

The Luchiano organization, my grandfather practically, had a huge problem with me being born and my father wanting to be involved in my life. My dad had to fight his own flesh and blood countless times over my mother and me. It got so serious, my mother and I was sent away for our safety, but I guess we didn't get far enough. My mother was eventually murdered in cold blood.

My father knew exactly who sent the hit, so he sent one right back and had his own father killed; that's how I knew to never cross my old man. He went on honor and code and, no matter who you were, if you broke it, you would be dealt with accordingly.

With no traffic heading back toward Staten Island and New Jersey, we made it back to the island in a timely manner. Before I got out the backseat to get into my car, my pops grabbed my arm.

"It's one more thing," he said.

I sat back in my seat and closed the door. "What's up?" I inquired.

"I have a mark for you, but it's no regular one," he announced.

He peaked my interest with that statement, so I waited for him to finish.

"Chadd's wife, Lyric, I need you to meet her and get close to her," he explained.

Once he informed me of what kind of mark it was, I already knew why he wanted her to become accessible. It also meant he had a very strong feeling Chadd was doing something he wasn't supposed to be doing. "I got it, papa," I assured him.

Before I exited the truck, he handed me an envelope that was sealed. I didn't need to see the contents inside to know what it was. It was Lyric's entire profile with all her information, down to her favorite snack to eat.

I finally got out the truck and got in my car. Resting the envelope on the passenger seat, I started up the engine and pulled off my father's compound at full speed. The quicker I got away from my pops' folks, the better.

Being around some of those muthafuckers that worked for my old man made me cringe; the way they envied me was sickening. When I was around the mob, I tried to keep my words to the bare minimum, I only spoke when spoken to. The way I was, I had no filter, and I could care less how my words came out. Most people said I was naturally aggressive, while I would say I was just a real ass nigga.

I was from Queensbridge in Queens, a place where it wasn't easy to be raised. My mother was offered almost a million times to move out of the hood and into a nice luxury place by my pops, but she wouldn't budge. She kept with the same ol' talk about not depending on a man and, if God forbid something was to happen to him, me and her would've landed right back in the hood.

So, growing up, I was back and forth between Queensbridge and Staten Island but, ninety percent of the time, I was in Queens with my moms, always making sure she was good.

Ring! Ring! Ring!

My phone started to ring, blurring through my car speakers. I peered at the name that popped up and saw it was my wife, Catteleya. "Yes, Cat," I answered the phone, calling her by her nickname.

"Hey, I woke up and saw you were gone. You okay?" she pried.

"I'm good, heading back to the crib now."

"Okay, see you in a bit," she said and hung up.

I shook my head in annoyance. Sometimes, I wondered why I even went through with our marriage; then, I remembered I low-key didn't have any other choice but to.

Catteleya was the daughter of a well-known cartel leader, Raphael De León. We met at a club in the city, eyed each other for most of the night, and finally spoke. Once thing led to another and we started messing around. Cat's father found out and wasn't happy she was fooling around in the streets and wasn't married. He got wind of who my father was and made it a big deal.

At the time, my pops was looking for a connect in Mexico to get his loads through. Cat's father was running a huge length of the border, so they came to an agreement. They did business while I married his daughter and, of course, my father didn't allow me to have any say in anything. Times like that, I had wished my mother was still alive. She would've torn my pops' head apart, not caring what status he held.

Beeeeep!

The car behind me held down on their horn, trying to get my attention to drive off. I was at a traffic light and, apparently, it turned green while I was deep in my thoughts. Instead of pulling off so the people behind me could get to wherever they were going, I stepped out my car and raised my middle finger at the nigga behind me. Just like I thought, he sat behind his wheel and did absolutely nothing. I jumped back in my vee and pulled off without a care in the world.

Not living too far away from my father's estate, I reached the house I shared with Cat about twenty minutes later. As I pulled in the gate and onto the driveway, I could see her shadow in the upstairs window being nosy. I rounded my driveway, parked, and got out the car.

Before I pushed the key in the hole and turned the knob, I took a deep breath because my home didn't feel like a home and, when I was outside, that's when I was my happiest.

When I opened the door and stepped inside, our maid, Luci, was passing by.

"Buenos días, jefe," she greeted me.

"Morning, Luci." I waved at her and headed straight for my man cave.

When I entered and closed the door, everyone knew better than to disturb me. Before settling, I poked my head back out and shouted to Luci to make me some breakfast. When she acknowledged that she heard me, I closed the door back, expecting to only be interrupted by Luci when the food was done.

Plopping down on the sofa, I ripped open the envelope and pulled out the stack of paper that was inside. Just as I banked on it, it was the chick Lyric's detailed profile. I started to skim through the pages instead of reading it word for word. I told myself I'd do that after I ate and got some rest. But, by the information I glanced at, she was thirty years old, an author, and stayed home most of the time.

The pictures that were included threw me off a bit. It had some with her smaller in size while others showed she had weight on her. That's when I started to actually read the notes, word for word. After reading over the descriptions for the photos, I understood she gained weight over time and the bigger size, or what we called bigger chicks, BBW, was her current physical size.

Looking at her pictures, there was no denying her beauty. She was a good-looking woman, and I couldn't help but wonder what the fuck she was doing with a dude like Chadd.

Knock! Knock!

Once I heard the knocks at the door, I automatically figured it was Luci with my food. "Come in!" I yelled.

Luci entered, holding a tray of food and drinks in her hands. The aroma spread around the room within seconds of her walking inside.

"That shit smells good," I complimented.

"Gracias, Señor, it is." She smiled brightly as she handed over the tray.

As fast as she came, she exited with the same speed, giving me my space to eat in peace. I sat the papers to the side and started to buss down my food; a nigga was starving.

After a few minutes had past, most of the food was already gone. I didn't play when it came to my stomach, which was why I couldn't stand the fact Cat's ass couldn't cook to save her life. My mother always told me to make sure I married someone who could make sure I was fed breakfast, lunch, and dinner, with snacks in between; if not, leave them where they were.

Before my ass knew it, my plate was clean and my glass of juice was empty. Letting out a loud burp that came from deep within, I stretched and knew it was time to go to sleep. I hadn't sleep since the day before because I was out handling business for my pops.

I stuffed the papers back into the envelope, walked to my safe that was built into the wall and placed it inside, making sure to lock it. I grabbed the tray and left out my den, handed it to Luci who was in the kitchen cleaning up, and made my way upstairs to get some much-needed rest.

When I walked into the bedroom, Cat was laced in this dope ass lingerie that left nothing for my imagination. I couldn't lie; Cat was a fine ass woman. Shit, she had to be for me to had been fucking her from the jump. Although her body was done, I wasn't the type to complain. She was gorgeous with long jet-black hair, perky breasts, slim waist, and a nice ass that they made sure to lift.

"Hi, papi," she cooed in her strong accent.

I stood in the doorway with low eyes and just stared at her lustfully. If I wasn't so damn tired, I would've already attacked her, but I just didn't have any sort of energy.

Sitting at the foot of the bed, she crawled behind me and started to massage my shoulders, something I needed, and it felt good as fuck.

"Cat, I'm sorry, baby girl, a nigga beat," I plead. "You could suck my dick though, help me relieve some stress," I persuaded, not really caring if she did or didn't.

"Selfish ass nigga," she snapped.

Cat hopped off the bed, grabbed her robe and wrapped it around her body. She started to talk shit in Spanish, and that's when I knew it was my que to leave.

It was the unnecessary nagging I couldn't take, especially when she knew what kind of life I lived. As a wife, she should've dropped to her knees, sucked me off and sent my ass to sleep until I was properly energized to dick her down. If I was her, I would've woken me up to some pussy but, no, she was too concerned with only her nut and well-being.

While she continued to rant, I simply got up and went into another room, locked the door, and took my ass to sleep. She must've forgotten who the fuck paid the bills in the house, and it damn sure wasn't her father.

Annoying ass bitch, I thought as I drifted off to sleep.

LYRIC

Although I found out about Chadd and Kayla, I had hopes we could've had dinner and a nightcap afterwards to spark what we used to have but, when the end of the night came, the same thing happened: nothing.

I knew deep down inside, he was only trying to be nice to me because he was feeling guilty about what he was doing and, of course, to throw me off. Any person knew when their significant other neglected them completely, it was someone else so to throw me off, especially after making fun of me the night before, he made up for it with a dinner date.

Chadd's ass knew good and well if I was to find out, have proof and want a divorce, I would walk away with all his hard earnings, so he was trying to play it smart while he had his cake and ate it too.

The next morning after I went to sleep tipsy and horny, I woke up and Chadd was already gone, which was normal for him. I remembered in the beginning when he would make sure to kiss me on my forehead and tell me he loved me before leaving out for work. Over time, things changed and he would tip toe around, claiming he didn't want to wake me. It took less than a few seconds to reassure your wife of your love before departing for the day, so she could go right back to sleep but, if I told him that, I was complaining about little shit.

I finally got myself out the bed and went into the bathroom to deal with my hygiene. As usual, I went downstairs and made my coffee. While preparing it to brew, a piece on the machine got stuck, so I kept trying to pull it out, only to break a nail.

"Ouch!" I screeched. "Fuck, fuck, fuck." I stuck my index finger in my mouth to relieve some of the pain.

Looking at my nail, it was all messed up, and I had a thing where my nails and toes were always on point. I loved to see my nails nicely done and I typed or wrote while working, so a broken design wasn't giving what it needed to give.

Totally forgetting about the coffee, I went for my phone and called up my nail tech, Tiffany. I found her contact and hit the call button.

"Heyyy, my favorite author," she sang into the phone when she answered.

"Hey, Tiff, how are you?" I asked.

"I'm good, girl, just grinding. What's up?"

"I just broke a nail," I whined.

"Oh shit, it's bad? Never mind, don't answer that. A scratch on your design is major to you," she joked. We both started laughing. "When can you come in?"

"Girl, I can come now," I stated in a serious tone.

"Okay, I have a client now and one after. Come for around one o'clock," she instructed me.

"Okay, boo, I'll see you then."

"Cool, bye." We hung up.

I looked at my phone and saw it was only ten fifteen a.m. Not wanting to work under those conditions, plus my finger was still throbbing, I decided to relax and read a book.

Browsing through my *to read books* on my kindle app, my finger landed on My Heart Belongs to a Dope Boy by Karma Monae. I snuggled myself between my comforter and pillows and tapped into another banger.

Being that the book was a page turner and I was a fast reader, I was completed with the novella right in time for me to start getting myself ready to head to the nail salon.

While I was getting dressed, my phone started to ring. I was praying it wasn't Tiffany saying she was canceling, but it wasn't. "Hello?" I answered.

"Hello, Mrs. Larson?" a man asked.

"Yes, who's speaking?" I raised an eyebrow.

"This is Kyle calling from Jeffery's Automotive; your car is ready for pick up," he informed me.

"Oh, okay, thank you so much. I'll be over in a moment," I told him excitedly.

Yes! I don't have to travel all around.

I put a pep in my step since I had to get my car before making my nail appointment. They weren't far from each other, thankfully.

Before I knew it, I was walking out the door and getting into the backseat of an Uber. Being mid-day and everyone was in work or school, there was no traffic, so I arrived at the shop fast, got my car, and headed over to Tiffany's.

One o'clock on the dot was the time I pulled into the parking lot of the mini plaza Tiffany's salon was located. I was happy I got there on time because I didn't need my appointment being pushed back. Stepping out my car, I walked up to the salon but, before I was able to open the door, someone beeped their horn and called out to me.

"Damn, ma, you nice and thick!" a guy driving by in the parking lot yelled out.

I started to blush because it had been a while since I got a compliment of any sort. With no words seeming to want to come out of my mouth, I just waved and shot him a shy smile, then made my way inside the salon.

"Lyriccc," Tiffany dragged my name as soon as I stepped foot in her presence.

"Wassup, boo?" I smiled, making my way further into the salon.

The place wasn't packed; it had about two girls getting their nails done while two were in the back having their feet worked on.

"Come on, let me get you started ASAP." She motioned

for me to sit down in front of her. "You want me to just fix this, or you want a whole new look for both hands?"

"Just fix it. I have to get back in and write; this definitely wasn't on my schedule," I sighed out loud and rested my free hand on my forehand.

"Okay, I got you."

Tiffany immediately started putting in work. She was great at what she did; that's why she'd always gotten my business. When I first moved to Staten Island from Brooklyn, it was a big change, even though it was just across the water. The island was a whole other world; that's why most people would say they weren't a part of the five boroughs of New York City.

It was hard finding a dope hairstylist and nail tech when I first moved, so I always went back home to Crown Heights, Brooklyn to get pampered properly. While shopping at Staten Island Mall, both Tiffany and I were at the register in a store. She saw my nails and loved them. She then went on to mention she was a nail tech and started showing me her work, so I took her card.

One day, I just didn't feel like driving all the way across the bridge, so I put aside my fear and went to her. Tiffany slayed my nails and left me speechless and, that day, she gained a client and I'd always been back ever since.

About twenty minutes later, my index fingernail was back intact and looking lovely.

"Thank you so much, baby." I gave her air kisses. I went into my purse and pulled out a hundred-dollar bill.

"Here, keep the change as a tip." I shot her a wink.

"Now, this is how you mutha fuckin tip someone!" she shouted and waved the hundred in the air.

To fix my nail, it was only twenty dollars, but I took in consideration her squeezing me in last minute, doing a great job and doing so at a fast pace, so I could get back to work.

"Girl, you a fool. Leave these people alone," I giggled.

"Mmmhmm, whatever. Thanks for always supporting a bitch." She smiled.

"And thank you for always being on point." I stood to my feet and grabbed my things. "I'll talk to you later," I told Tiffany, as she cleaned up her station.

"Later, boo." She waved, as I exited out the salon.

The time was creeping to two o'clock, so I swiftly walked to my car, so I could beat the afternoon traffic of people getting off work and school. Plus, I was far behind in my word count goal for the day. I had a lot of catching up to do when I got inside.

As soon as I got in the car, I cranked it up and pulled out.

Bang!

"Oh, my fuckin' God!" I screamed out. "I just got my car back!"

Not wasting a second, I hopped out the car and walked up to the driver side of the other vehicle. Approaching them, the driver's door swung up and a tall, brown-skin, handsome ass man stepped out.

"So, you just pull out without looking?" he snapped.

"You came out of nowhere; you didn't see me pulling out?" I retorted.

"Shorty, I have the right of way. How do you even sound?" he stated, scrunching up his face.

We both walked over to where the cars collided. The damage wasn't as bad, but the scratches were still noticeable, especially since both of our cars were foreign models. Mine, a 2022 black Mercedes-Benz C Class and, his, a 2022 black Porsche Cayenne.

"So, who paying for this?" I sassed. "I literally just got my car out the shop an hour ago," I informed him, even though he probably didn't give a shit.

"Listen, I don't have time for the back and forth or even getting on the line with my insurance. My family own a shop; they can get both our cars fixed up in no time. You can follow me if you want," he stated and started to walk back to the driver side of his car.

"Oh, wait, wait. While that sounds nice and all, I can't go right now. I have to get back home to write." I stopped him in his tracks.

"Write?" He raised an eyebrow.

"I'm an author, and I'm behind on my work for the day, so can we choose another, well, for my car that is," I plead.

He looked at me with a blank look for a minute before speaking again. "Aight, shorty. Take my math and hit my line when you ready," he volunteered.

I turned around and opened the passenger side door to my car, reached inside and grabbed my phone. "What's your number?" I asked, walking back up to him.

"347-919-0130," he recited, then went to get in his car.

Wait, what the hell is his name? I asked myself.

As he was getting ready to pull off, I waved him down, so he rolled down his window.

"What's good?" he asked.

"I didn't get your name."

"It's Lo," he simply said, whined back up his glass and peeled off.

Rude ass nigga.

CHAPTER 7

LOGAN

After I woke up from getting some much-needed rest, I got right down to work. I studied her profile from front to back. I learned everything I needed to learn and made sure to keep the important things in the front of my head; for example, Chadd was cheating on her with his assistant.

At the time, I was unaware if she knew or had an idea. If she did, I knew it would've been an easy way in for me. If she didn't and she was a solid chick, it would've been hard to break her down. No job was too hard for me though, just would've had to put in some extra work, that was all.

As soon as I finished her file, I called in a tail, that's how I knew where to find her and cause the minor accident. I wasn't wasting no time; I had a job to get done.

Once our little run-in was over, I pulled out of the parking lot feeling confident. Phase one of my plan was completed and it went smooth. Once I drove off, I turned up my music and let my guy Pop Smoke, may his soul rest in peace, snap on the track I was playing.

I was headed straight to the repair shop that my family owned to get my Porsche buffed and painted over. Even though I could've banged the car up and went and bought a whole new one the same day, I didn't. I had to make sure and keep up the act.

I pulled into the garage and, as soon as I stepped out of my car, one of the workers approached me.

"Lo, what can we do for you today?" he asked.

"I need that to look new again," I said, pointing to the scratch and dent on the side of my car.

"No problem, I'll get on that now," he assured me. "Tony!" he yelled for another worker.

"Yo, my Uncle Frank in his office?" I grabbed his attention before he walked off.

"Yeah, he's in," he informed me.

"Good lookin'." I nodded and headed in the direction of my uncle's office in the back.

My phone chimed, letting me know I had a text message. Unlocking it, I pulled down the notifications and saw it was a message from one of my little side joints.

Candi: When you're free, come through, I'm trying to show you something

I smirked at the message because I knew damn well she wasn't lying. Candi been around for a while; she knew how to please a nigga and knew her place. I never had to worry about her running her mouth or nagging me, but I still didn't trust her. In my line of work and the type of family I was a part of, trust was hard to come around.

Me: Say less

I never told her the exact day or time I was coming; it was just safer that way. I'd just pull up and tell her open the door. Most times, she was on deck while on a few occasions, she wasn't home, and I just had to chalk it up as bad timing.

Knock! Knock!

"Unc!" I yelled to the other side of the door.

"Come in," I heard him say.

I walked in the plush office, which many would have thought was a bit much for an automotive owner's office but, if you knew my family, you would know why it was the way it was.

"Wassup, Uncle Frank," I greeted him as I made my way inside the office.

"Nephew, what's the deal?" He smiled brightly.

Uncle Frank was my father's older brother and best friend. He was damn near like a second father to me, something I thought my grandfather would've been. Initially, Frank was supposed to be the head of the organization, but my grandfather and the other members that sat at the table felt my pops was a better fit for the position. My uncle was wild and didn't give a fuck; he didn't think before he spoke or acted, which made him get into a lot of bullshit. Everyone said I reminded them of him.

"Shit, had to bring my car to get smoothed out, had a lil' accident," I told him.

"Oh, ok, ok. How's everything besides that? You good?"

"Yeah, I'm cooling, Unc, you know me." I took a seat across from him while he sat at his desk.

He sat back in his seat and nodded his head with a smile on his face. If it was one person on my father's side of the family that loved every bone in my body, it was my Uncle Frank. He would bat for me no matter what, just as hard as my pops would and, for that, I was always appreciative of him and would drop a nigga in a heartbeat over him.

"What your father have you doing now a days?" He rocked in his chair.

"Got me getting close to a mark's wife, easy shit." I shrugged.

"Never underestimate an assignment, especially when it's a woman. They are deadly and I'm not speaking on violence," he schooled me.

Even though it was my first time having to get close to a female, I didn't think too much of it. When my uncle started to drop gems on the game, I took heed because it was always a reason why he said what he said.

"I got chu'," I assured him.

We continued to chop it up about random shit, had food ordered and just chilled until my car was completed and dry. Ready to dip, I said my farewells for the time being and decided to head over to Candi's spot.

I called up my second set of eyes, Joe, so he would survey the area before I got to Candi and stay until I left. I had a certain routine I did when going to see females. I wasn't the type to get caught slippin'. I didn't have beef in the streets but, because of my affiliation, I was always a target.

As I got near Candi's crib, I called Joe.

"Yeah, Lo," he answered on the first ring.

"Everything quiet over there?" I inquired.

"Yeah, nothing moving, you good."

"Bet," I simply said and hung up.

Moments later, I arrived at her spot. I passed by Joe parked up and found a parking spot near him. I saw her car outside, so I knew she was home and, the way she spoke earlier that day, I knew she would've been. I pressed the call button next to her name.

"Hey, Lo," she sang into the phone.

"Wassup? Come open the door," I instructed her.

Without uttering a word, she hung up and appeared in her doorway seconds later.

Yeah, she want the D, I laughed to myself.

As I walked up her front porch, I shot Joe a head nod and, before I closed the door behind me, I looked in his direction again to see him blink his lights, giving me an extra reassurance.

"I guess I wasn't the only one who needed a fix," she teased as she switched her ass side to side on her way into her living room.

"Man, what you talkin' 'bout?" I chuckled, taking a seat on the sofa.

She stepped between my legs and squatted down. Although her ass was facing in the opposite direction, I knew it was out on full display because she only wore a t-shirt, which wasn't even big enough to cover her body.

Candi had a dope ass body that made a nigga brick up in seconds looking at her naked; she wasn't a great looker, but she also wasn't butt ass ugly. While I fucked different broads on different occasions, I was never the type of nigga to have them in positions that I would have my wife or someone I cared about. Candi was one of those bitches I just fucked and nothing more.

"I'll show you what I'm talking about," she giggled as she pulled down my Nike sweats and my boxer briefs.

Candi wasn't into wasting time, so my dick was in her mouth the moment it touched the air. I leaned back and enjoyed the warmth of her mouth, as she jerked, sucked, and took me to another world.

"Mmm," she moaned while licking my balls.

"Fuck, shorty," I blurted out.

The way she did her thing with her tongue, shit made my toes curl in my Jordan's. "Come sit on it," I ordered.

Taking one last long suck, she kissed the head of my dick and stood up. I pulled a condom from my sweats on the ground and handed it to her. Knowing exactly what to do, she ripped the pack, slid the condom down my tool and, within seconds, she turned around so her back was facing me and dropped right down onto my lap.

"Damnnn, Lo!" she cried out.

I grabbed her waist to help guide her up and down while

I thrusted upwards, making sure to get deep in her pussy. Candi continued to cry out in pleasure, as I dug her guts on. Enjoying the pain, she started to throw her ass back, making it bounce all around.

Not being able to contain myself, I slapped her right cheek real hard, leaving a red handprint on her light-skinned body. Pushing her forward a bit, I stood up and bent her over with my dick still inside. Candi knew how to take every inch of me. Even if certain positions would hurt, she happily took the pain and let me do me.

I continued to fuck her from behind until I felt myself coming to a climax. Grabbing a handful of hair, I pulled her towards me, making her arch her back more while I dumped my load into the condom.

Once emptied, I slowly pulled out and sat back on the sofa to catch my breath. Candi turned around with a bright smile on her face and walked off towards the bathroom.

My phone started to ring. Thinking it was someone important, I looked at it, but it was only Cat. "Yo," I answered and took a deep breath.

"I haven't spoken to you all day, wassup with you?" she whined.

"Cat, not right now," I told her nonchalantly.

"Why? You with one of your bitches?"

"Yeah, I am. Now, go be with one of your niggas," I spat and hung up the phone. I wasn't always a dickhead, especially to her, but some things happened and it turned me cold.

After some time in our marriage, I caught Cat cheating

with some nigga I knew she was fooling around with while I was dicking her down. But once our marriage was sealed, I tried my best to give it a chance but, apparently, she didn't.

Before I had a chance to kill him myself, her father sent a hit out to kill him. She strongly believed it was me who killed him and, while I had planned on doing so, I didn't appreciate the way she expressed her rage, like she wasn't the one cheating. If her hot ass loved him for real, she should've married him before her father found out about her indulging in sexual acts before marriage. I wouldn't have had to deal with her at all.

"Fuck you, Logan!" she shouted.

Candi was walking back towards me with a washcloth in hand. She bent down, waited for me to slip the condom off and wiped me clean. "You good, daddy?" Candi asked as she finished.

"Yeah, good lookin'."

"Wow, you're really fucked up. Go be with your lil' bitch," Cat gritted.

"I will, at least she ain't annoying and disloyal," I simply said and hung up on her dumbass.

It was the truth. All my hoes knew what it was. I ain't have no stress coming from them; but, Cat, shorty was a whole different ball game.

Maybe she'll change, or maybe not, I thought.

CHAPTER 8

LYRIC

After the small accident I had with the dude, Lo, I rushed home to open my laptop and get to work. Even though I was somewhat blocked mentally, I had to push through to catch up since I was behind on schedule. While trying to focus, my phone rang with my mother's picture popping up on the screen.

"Hi, ma," I answered on the first ring, so I could get this conversation done and over fast.

Anytime I was in crunch mode, it seemed as though it was when everyone wanted to speak to me or do something the most. While I was free and on my little break in between books, my phone was dryer than the Sahara Desert.

"Lyric, baby, how are you?" she sang.

"I'm good, just working, same ol'," I answered.

"How's Chadd? I have to come across the water and visit soon since you act like you don't want to come over this way."

"Ma, it's not that. I've just been focused on building my brand and catalog, so it's been tough. I barely go out in general. Ask Chadd, I'm always home," I plead.

It wasn't a lie. Ninety-five percent of the time, I was in the house while the other five percent, I'd pop outside just to get my hair and nails done or to grocery shop.

"I understand, love, but please try to make some time for us over here. I miss you a lot."

If you miss me so much, why don't you make time like Lori-Ann do? I thought to myself but knew better than to speak those words.

"Will do Mommy," I sympathized.

"Good, I'll let you get back to writing. Be good, baby, love you."

"I love you more, lady."

We finally hung up.

I was raised in Crown Heights, Brooklyn, right on Troy and Bergen in Albany Projects. A lot of people said I got lucky when I married Chadd because I got up out the hood but, little did they know, I held my own weight since I was in high school.

Whenever I went home, I was treated like a little celebrity, the big author that's always making the New York Time's Best Selling list. While there were people who appreciated my grind and was sincerely happy for me, there were individuals who envied me, talked shit, and always threw shade my way like we didn't all have the same twenty-four hours.

Not really having a legit reason to go back home, besides my mom, I just chose to stay away. Why would I waste my precious little me time I did get to go be around people who would turn up their nose at me or have their hands out? My mother was always welcomed to my home, and she knew that; that's all that mattered.

Shaking off the negative thoughts, I dove right back into writing. My character was talking to me, finally, and I had to get her words out my head and onto my manuscript. Turning my phone on *do not disturb*, I had a great rest of my writing session. No interruptions, and the story started to flow again, allowing me to catch up on my word count goal.

Finally, completed with my writing for the day, it was about eight o'clock at night. I checked my phone for any messages since I had it on DND, but there wasn't anything but social media notifications. I went on and checked them and found myself looking at my memories. A picture of Kayla, Chadd, his friend, and co-worker John and me popped up.

Hmmm, look at this shit here.

Seeing Kayla triggered something in me. I'd been cool and calm about the situation, trying my best to put on a front and play like I had no clue about their affair, but it wasn't easy. Images of Chadd and Kayla popped into my head, making me even more upset. I looked at the time and saw Chadd should've definitely been home already. I decided to call him and see what he was doing.

The first time, it rang out and went to voicemail. The second time, it just went straight to voicemail. My heart started to race as my fingers twitched, wanting to text him some mess, but I knew it wouldn't end well; that's when I told myself I was going to call Kayla to see if she heard from him, since she was his assistant and all.

Ring! Ring! Ring!

She didn't answer the first time around, but I called again, and she did.

"Hello?" she answered with hesitance in her voice.

"Hi, Kayla, do you know where Chadd is?" I cut straight to the chase.

"Yes, he's at a dinner meeting with a client. He didn't tell you?" she questioned.

Nope, just like he ain't tell me he was fucking you.

"No, he must've forgot to mention it to me," I concluded.

"Men," she said and started laughing.

"Right, men," I agreed. "How have you been? We haven't spoken or saw each other in a while. Everything good?" I pried.

"Oh, everything is great, girl. I hope all is well on your end," she cooed.

"Yeah, it is," I simply said. It wasn't in me to allow her any comfort in knowing my hurt and pain. As far as she knew, I was still happy in my marriage, even though she was getting dicked down.

"That's great."

"Well, I'll talk to you later. If you speak to Chadd before I do for any reason, let him know to contact me as soon as possible," I insisted.

"Sure thing, love."

"Take care now, bye."

"Bye," she sang happily and hung up.

I can't believe this hoe.

It was unbelievable how she played that shit off so well. Kayla spoke to me in the same way she usually would. It had me thinking if she was dealing with Chadd since they'd met, and I was blind the entire time. While the Brooklyn in me wanted to show out, I talked myself down because I couldn't let them know I was on to them; it would ruin my whole plan of gaining evidence. Speaking of evidence, I was still waiting for the video from Mrs. Lawrence.

To relax myself, I did what I always found to work, take a nice hot bath. Once I was finished with that, I dove straight into the bed. I was beat and couldn't care less where Chadd was in that moment in time.

***

THE BIRDS CHIRPING a sweat melody outside my windows woke me up the following morning. When I cracked my eyes open, I didn't feel that heaviness in my eyelids, which told me I had gotten a goodnight's rest.

I turned over to see Chadd wasn't sleeping next to me or was his side of the bed slept on, once again. Shaking my head in annoyance and aggravation, I rolled out of bed and went on my journey to find him, that was if he was even in the house. Not having to look too far, when I passed the closest guestroom to our bedroom, I saw him cuddled up in between the blankets and pillows.

Looking at the window, the sun was already up and to see him still fast asleep was weird. Chadd usually would get up while the world was still resting to get ready for work. He was always out the door and on his way to Manhattan before other cars started to hit the road.

Then, it hit me. Kayla did say he had a dinner meeting, which could've gone down the road of drinking his life away. He used to do that here and there if he felt stressed. That's if he was even at a damn meeting. Kayla could've been telling me anything and he was right there next to her, coaching her on what to say.

Shaking the two from my mind, I went downstairs to make myself a cup of coffee but, when I got there, it wasn't any left to make. Sighing out loud, I started looking around the kitchen to see what else we were low on. If I didn't pay attention to stuff like that in the house, we would've stayed without certain things. After taking note of what was needed, I went back upstairs to get ready to make a grocery run while it was still early.

About forty minutes later, my hygiene was in place, and I was dressed and walking out the door while Chadd was still asleep. As I was about to make it over to the driver side of my car, I remembered the scratch on the passenger side, so I went over to look at it.

Frustrated all over again, I rolled my eyes and got in the car. Before pulling out the driveway, I scrolled through my contacts and landed on the dude's, Lo, name and hit the call button. It rang a few times before he answered.

"Who this?" he answered all aggressively with his deep voice.

"Hi, ummm, good morning. It's Lyric," I spoke into the phone.

"Lyric who?" he turned and asked with a hint of annoyance in his tone.

"The woman you hit yesterday," I retorted.

He started to chuckle, making me confused.

"What's funny?"

"You mean the woman who don't know how to look both ways before pulling out. Yeah, I know who you are, what's good?" he jested.

"Whatever you say. Is that offer still on the table for me to get my car taken care of? I hate the look of it; it's irritating my eyes," I expressed.

"Yeah, when can you bring it by?"

"Is sometime today cool?" I pushed. I just wanted to get it over and done with.

"Yeah, it won't take long either, so you'll be able to get back to your writing," he emphasized.

"Ha, ha, very funny," I let out a fake laugh.

"Yeah, aight, shorty. I'll text you the address. What time you sliding?" he questioned.

"Is two o'clock good?"

"Whenever you want," he offered.

"Okay, two it is. I'll text you when I'm on my way," I informed him.

"Aight, bet. I'ma holla at you then," he said before hanging up.

That was set. I was going to be able to go to the grocery shop and return home to write for a good bit before heading back out to deal with the car. Finally, I put my car in reverse, backed out the driveway and went about my business.

As usual, I was in and out of the supermarket within an hour. I made a list of the things I needed and stuck to it. Had I had went to Target or Walmart, it would've been a different story; my ass would've been in there buying something from every department.

I got back home and unpacked everything. Finally able to get my morning dose of coffee, I was ready to work. For a few hours, I sat behind my laptop while my fingers went a hundred miles per hour. Chadd was already gone by the time I returned home, so I had no distractions.

Some hours later and four thousand words typed, I felt satisfied at the pace I was going. I looked at the time on my laptop and saw I had to start heading out to the shop. Quickly putting the address in my phone's maps to make sure I wasn't going to be behind schedule, I saw it was only twenty minutes away.

Good, because I need to be in and out.

I shot Lo a quick text message.

Me: I'm leaving out the house now, should be there in the next twenty minutes

Still dressed in a sweatsuit from earlier that morning, I grabbed my things, including my laptop, and jetted out the door. By the time I got in the car, my phone binged, letting me know I had message. I hit the button on the side to preview it.

Lo: Aight cool, I'll be there

After getting the confirmation from him, I pulled out and was on my way to the shop, arriving in the exact amount of time the GPS said. When I pulled up, I saw his Porsche, so I knew he was there. While in the process of calling him, I looked up before hitting the call button and saw him walking towards my car, so I rolled down my window.

"You gon' stay in the car while they do it or you getting out?" he asked sarcastically.

"Good afternoon to you too," I retorted, rolling my eyes.

"Man, we spoke this morning. Come on, so these people can do their job," he demanded, motioning me to get out the car.

While I was confused on who he thought he was talking to, I was also a bit turned on. Although Chadd was my husband and of course the man of the house, he never gave off that Alpha male vibe but, Lo, he did. Lo had this way about him. He moved like a boss, like he owned everything around him. Lo gave off that vibe that if it wasn't his way, it would've been the highway.

"I'm coming." I smacked my lips as I grabbed my laptop bag, purse, and phone. "Calm down," I mumbled under my breath, which he didn't hear.

As I got out the car, some of the workers eyed me, letting their focus linger a little too long for my comfort, but what the hell? It was the only attention I'd gotten in a minute, so I didn't make it an issue.

Following Lo, I noticed we were headed for his car. "Ummm, where we going?" I stopped in my tracks.

"You want to stay here while they work on your car, or you want to go grab something to eat in the meantime?" He raised his brows.

"I mean I was going to write while they—" I looked at his facial expression and stopped my sentence. Lifting my foot one after the other, I continued to walk behind him. "Ughhh, whatever," I sighed.

I climbed in his Porsche, which was exceptionally clean and comfortable, rested my laptop between my feet, purse on my lap and sat back. As soon as he started up the car, he speed off from the shop to a destination that was unknown to me.

"Where are we going exactly?" I quizzed.

He continued to look forward and drive, leaving silence between us and only music to be heard. For a second, I started to freak out because at the end of the day, Lo was a complete stranger and not knowing where we were headed made me uneasy.

A few moments later, we pulled into the parking lot of a well-known diner. He looked over at me with a grin on his face, then returned his attention to finding a parking spot. Once I saw we were in a public place, I loosened up and relaxed in the passenger seat. He found a spot to park near the entrance. We hopped out and went inside.

"Good afternoon, welcome to Hylan Diner. Would you

like a booth, or you prefer sitting at the bar?" the host greeted us.

Lo looked over at me to answer the question.

"Ah, I guess a booth is okay," I blurted out.

"Follow me this way," he stated, and we did just that.

We were seated at the end booth, away from most of the other patrons. It didn't matter to me either way because it wasn't like we were on a date and wanted to get to know each other.

As soon as I sat down, I took my laptop out and cracked it open.

"So, you really finna write right now?" He raised an eyebrow.

"I mean, you paying my bills?" I retorted.

"Nah, but whoever put that ring on your finger should be." He pointed to my wedding ring.

"He doing what he needs to do, but I like my own money." I curled up my lip at him.

"I get it, I respect it." He held his hands up in surrender.

If on que, the waitress approached our table to take our orders. While he spoke to her, I couldn't help but notice his handsome features. He was indeed black but was also defi-nitely mixed with something; he had an exotic look to him. Lo had hazel eyes, a straight nose, thick eyebrows, fade hair-cut, with a properly trimmed and shaped beard. He was tall, about six-two or so, and his swag was something serious. He knew how to dress and, even simply in a sweatsuit, anyone could see that.

"Yo, what you getting?" he asked, pulling me from me trance.

"Oh, umm, let me just get a strawberry milkshake. I ate before I left the house," I lied.

I didn't want to eat in front of a stranger. I barely liked to eat in front of Chadd with his judgmental ass, so I didn't need another man looking at me crazy while I tried to enjoy my meal.

"You sure?" he asked.

"Yeah." I shot him a shy smile.

The waitress confirmed the orders and ran off to fill them. I got on my laptop to check my emails while he had his face down in his phone; we did that until the food and my shake came. The entire time, we barely spoke; he seemed to be wrapped up into whatever it was on his phone, but I wasn't mad. We were just killing time while my car was being worked on.

"Must be an interesting conversation," I blurted out.

He looked at me confused, shooting me a look like, *what are you talking about?*

"You haven't removed your eyes from your phone since we sat down," I pointed out.

"Okay, so? You been behind your screen too; you don't see me saying shit to you," he attested.

"You know what, you're right. Let me mind my business." I refocused back on my laptop.

I wish I was able to write, but it was too much going on in the diner for me to concentrate. I either needed peace and quiet or music playing and, at that moment, I was unable to get neither.

"You checked in with your husband?" Lo came out and asked randomly.

"Why does it matter? I'm a grown ass woman and I'm not doing anything," I voiced.

"Never said you were but, if you was my wife, I don't care if you were going to the corner store, I want to know."

"Sounds controlling and I'm not, so no worries for you." I shot him a wink.

"I guess so, ma," he chuckled and returned his gaze on his phone.

In between time, I caught him looking at me but didn't think nothing of it. A guy like him would never go for a woman like me. He looked like the type to have a bunch of bad bitches swarming him on a daily; I didn't stand a chance.

When I realized I even had those thoughts, I cursed myself because I was a married woman; I shouldn't care if I stood a chance with another man or not.

"Your car is ready," he informed me, snapping me out of my thoughts.

"Oh, good," I said happily.

I packed away my things while he called for the check. I pulled out a twenty-dollar bill to pay for my shake, but he quickly slid it back towards me.

"I got it," he assured me.

"It's okay, Lo, I can pay for my own shake."

"I know you can, but my mother told me as a man, you should always pick up the tab."

He went ahead and paid the waitress and left a tip as well. When he stood to his feet, I followed his lead, as we exited out the diner and got into his car. Not long after, we were back at the shop but, as we pulled up, Lo looked hesitant to get out the car but eventually did.

There was a Hispanic woman who looked gorgeous as ever standing with a scowl on her face as we exited the car.

"Who the hell is this?" she asked with on hand on her hip and the next pointing in my direction.

"Cat, please don't get me tight," Lo said in a calm manner.

"I got a call about you out with some broad, so don't tell me shit about getting tight because I'm already there."

"Get in your car and go home," he ordered her.

"What the hell is going on out here?" an older man appeared out of nowhere and asked.

Looking at his features and by his accent, I knew he was Italian.

"Unc, my fault, I'll handle it," Lo turned and said.

Oh, uncle? He did say this was his family's shop, I thought.

It all made sense to me in that moment. I knew Lo was mixed with something. He was Italian and black; his uncle confirmed it.

"Yeah, do that. And, Cat, you know better than to come up in here acting the fool," he grilled her.

I just stood there while everything was going on. I was lost and had no part in anything. Lo was so heated; I saw it written all over his face. He walked back to his car, got in and sped off, leaving all of us there. Immediately after, the woman hopped in her vehicle but, before pulling off, she eyed me closely.

"Here's your keys ma'am," one of the workers said as he handed me my car keys.

I took it from him and looked at my car. They did a damn good job. It looked brand new to me, like there was never an accident. "Thank you, how much do I owe?" I started to grab my wallet.

"Nothing, everything was handled," he informed me.

"Ummm, okay. Thank you," I spoke hesitantly.

I got in my car, and Lo popped right into my head. Of course, he was the one who paid for my car. I told myself I had to either call or text him to let him know I was appreciative, but it wasn't the right time. He was definitely occupied.

Wait, was that his wife or joint? I thought as I pulled off.

LOGAN

If it was any other chick I was out with, I wouldn't had given a fuck, but Cat literally could've potentially fucked up my whole plan. She acted off of impulse and always failed to realize that.

When I left Uncle Frank's, I drove straight home because I knew she was following me. Literally, moments after I pulled onto our estate, she did as well. I walked in the house and purposely closed the door behind me. The longer it took for her to be in my presence, the better it was for her.

"Really? You're being petty as fuck, closing the door knowing damn well I'm right behind you!" Cat shouted when she walked inside the house.

I turned around, bent the corner, and walked up on her,

making her take a couple steps back into the wall. "What type of weird timing you on, yo?" I fumed.

"What you mean? You're the one who was caught with a bitch, not me," she threw in my face.

"Bro—"

I stopped talking because I knew it was only seconds before I ended up hurting her feelings. Plus, I knew better than to talk too much when it came to the business at hand.

"Cat, she was only a friend that I was helping out. Nothing more, nothing less," I spoke calmly.

"So, why didn't you just say that from jump?"

"You didn't give me a chance. You came out there wilding and shit, embarrassing me."

"I'm sorry." She lowered her head. "I started thinking the worse because I was trying to reach you and I couldn't. Then, one of my friends called me and told me they saw you and some chick getting in your car at your uncle's shop," she went on to explain.

Nosy ass bitches.

"Everything ain't always as they seem," I stated and walked away but was quickly stopped.

"My papa is coming in today. He'll be here for dinner and mentioned something about see you is imperative," she announced.

I turned around to see her facial expression serious; she wasn't cappin'. Her father barely crossed the border and, when he did, it was serious business. I had no idea what he was coming for. As far as I knew, everything between our families and business were intact.

"Aight, let me know when he's here. I'm about to go rest for a bit. Make sure the cook makes your father's favorite," I told her before walking up the stairs to go to the bedroom.

I stripped out of my clothes, slid in bed, and was knocked out before I was even able to count a sheep.

———

A SOFT HAND massaged my shoulder, waking me out of my slumber. I raised my head a little, opened one eye and saw it was Cat.

"He's on his way," she simply stated.

"Mmmhmmm." I laid my head back down on the pillow. I felt her get off the bed and leave out the room.

Rolling over, I stretched and tried to wake myself up. For the last couple days, my sleeping pattern had been all over the place. I just needed one good day of rest, no dealing with an annoying wife, not doing anything for my pops, not even entertaining my hoes, just sleep.

Dragging my hand around the bed, I felt for my phone. Finally locating it, I checked to see if Lyric had texted or call me, but she didn't. I just prayed Cat little stunt didn't fully scare her off completely, even though she had no reason to have to speak to me since her car was taken care of.

Mustering up enough energy, I got out the bed and went into the bathroom to get myself together for dinner with De León. Making sure to move at a fast pace, I was dressed and awaiting his arrival. I wouldn't have heard the last if he'd reached here and I was still getting ready, from both him and Cat.

While I waited in my man cave, I continued to study addition information I got on Chadd and Lyric. There were some pages on his mistress, Kayla. After reading through it, I found she was one trifling ass hoe.

Lyric basically befriended her, got her a job working for Chadd, and she turned around and slept with her husband. Women were real catty. Whatever they wanted, they'd go for it no matter who it hurt in the process.

Knock! Knock!

I heard someone at the door. "Yeah!" I shouted over the music I had playing.

"Mr. De León is here, jefe," Luci informed me.

"Okay."

Putting up the paperwork, I placed it back into my safe and made my way outside to greet him. Cat met me halfway, as we both approached the door. When we opened it, her father was stepping out of the SUV he was transported in.

"Papi!" Cat squealed once she laid eyes on her father.

Why the fuck you don't get like that when you see me? I thought.

"Doll face, hi, my baby," De León exclaimed as he made his way up the stairs to us.

The two embraced, as I sat back and waited my turn. Once they were finished their introduction, he turned me to him and pulled me in by one hand for a strong embrace.

"Yerno, cómo estás?" he asked.

"Bueno, bueno." I tapped his back. "Let's get inside." I motioned for him to enter the house.

His bodyguards divided amongst themselves, some stayed outside while two came inside with us.

"Luci!" De León sang when he saw her.

"Hola, Mr. De León," she greeted him.

The two hugged like they were old friends. Luci been in Cat's life for a while, before we even met, so she had history with the family.

We all went into the dining room and took our respective seats, me at the head of the table and Cat next to me. She gave up her seat across from me out of respect to her father. I, on the other hand, would never give up my seat for the next man, not even my father.

Not long after, the cook and his workers were coming out of the kitchen with our plates, resting them down in front of us.

"Here is the night's appetizers, enjoy," the chef said and exited the dining room.

It was Tacos al pastor, one of my favorites. Almost immediately, everyone dug right in and ate their foods. Following the appetizer, they brought out the entrée that was Chicken Mole, De León's favorite.

We ate, sipped on wine, talked, and caught up on everything, mostly family matters. We never spoke business in front of Cat; it was an unwritten rule to not involve the women in serious affairs as such.

Before I knew it, dinner was over, the jokes were finished,

and it was time for her father and I to go into my den and discuss whatever matter he had brought with him.

Pouring him a shot of Tequila, I did the same for myself. I handed it over to him once he got comfortable in his seat. We knocked glasses and took it to the head, accepting the burning sensation that came with it.

"I hear your father is out of the country," he spoke up.

"Yeah, he'll be back very soon, though. Everything okay?" I inquired.

"Yes, yes, everything is fine." He waved over one of his guards and whispered something in his ear, which made him exit the room.

"So, what's up with the surprise visit?" I asked, not trying to beat around the bush.

"Well, I wanted to check in on my princess and her prince, secondly—"

His guard walked back into the room but with two duffle bags in each hand. "I need you to take care of this for me. Your father said to bring it to you." He pointed to the two bags.

"Oh, did he? What did he say exactly?" I eyed the size of the bags; I knew it was a lot of money in it.

"He said he have an investor and for you to take it to him," he went on.

Why would he want me to take this money to the same person he has suspicion about?

"Let me give him a quick call." I lifted my finger up, letting him know to give me a minute.

Calling my pops, he answered on the third ring on his WhatsApp number.

"Logan," he answered.

"Ciao, papa," I greeted him. "Am I supposed to visit the investor to pay two invoices?" I asked him in a discreet way.

They say WhatsApp was encrypted, but we never fully trusted anything, not in our line of work and not with our last name.

"Yes," he answered.

"Alright, I'll handle it."

The line went dead, and I returned my attention back to Cat's father. "How much is it in total?" I queried.

"Four million," he articulated.

Yeah, just bring four fuckin' mill to my crib for me to transport randomly, I thought.

Now, showing my frustration or annoyance of the situation, I simply just told him, "Okay."

Since dinner went smooth and business was handled, the night was coming to an end. De León left as fast as he came, and Cat and I returned back to our normal lives of not being a happy couple.

As I was kicking back in the den, my phone vibrated once, letting me know it was only a text message.

Lyric: Thank you for taking care of my car and covering the cost, you didn't have to. Let me at least make it up to you some way, so I don't feel like I was given something. Anyway, I hope everything has settled on your end, have a goodnight.

Just the text I needed to receive. I was still in the ball game.

THE MOON SWITCHED out with the sun, and it was a new day. I had one thing on my agenda, and it was to visit Chadd at his place of business. I was low-key excited to go see that nigga. I wanted to finally be able to feel him out myself, one on one and not in passing like when we were introduced. I called Joe and had him prepare himself to make the run with me. By the time I was ready, he was outside waiting for me.

"Aye, Luci, go outside and tell Joe come grab these duffle bags and put them in the trunk of the SUV," I instructed her.

Since it was a large amount of faces, I couldn't take the risk of just driving in my car with Joe. Not only did I have to worry about a clown ass nigga possibly making me a target, but I also had to worry about twelve pulling me over and trying to search the car. How would I have explained four mill in duffle bags just sitting in my trunk?

Before I even decided on calling in extra eyes, ears, and guns, my father had already sent over some men. So, we were rolling three trucks deep, but Joe was my right hand in the situation.

When I got outside, Joe had just finished putting the bags in the truck, so we both hopped in, and all three vehicles pulled off my compound and was on our way to Manhattan with some of the deadliest men guarding us, including myself.

Leaving after the traffic died down was smart; we got there in no time. The only thing I wasn't so happy about was dealing with this shit during the day. I liked to move late and low, but my father wanted me to make an appearance at the top of the morning, so that's what I did. I never questioned his logic; he had a reason for doing things a certain way.

"Chadd Larson, please," I told the receptionist.

She got right on the phone and contacted him, or so I thought. Seconds later, the chick Kayla walked out into the waiting area.

"Hi, I'm Kayla, Mr. Larson's assistant." She stuck her hand out for me to shake.

His assistant alright.

Instead of extending my hand, I just looked down at hers. She quickly caught on and pulled back her hand.

"I don't have you on his schedule. Wait, what's your name?" she went on babbling.

"Miss, do me a favor and just tell him Luchiano is here," I told her sternly.

She went to the receptionist's desk and made a call. As soon as she mentioned the name, her face turned very serious. "Follow me," she instructed as she made her way from back around the desk and towards the door she came out from.

Joe and I followed her to the back with the bags in hand. When we reached Chadd's office, he was just finishing up with a call. His face when he saw me told that he was scared shitless.

"Kayla, I have it from here," he told her. "M-Mr.- Luchiano, what can I do for you?" he stuttered.

She exited out the office, leaving all three of us alone.

"My old man told me to drop these to you." Joe and I tossed the bags onto the ground and took a seat.

Chadd got up from his chair behind his desk and took a look at the bags. "How much is that?" he asked, pointing at them.

"Four mill."

"Four mill, on a random drop off, during the daytime?" He held his head.

I was enjoying the stress that came over him. He looked like he didn't know what to do but, little did he know, it was all a test.

"I'm going to have to go about this another way. I'll fill your father in," he mentioned.

"Mmmhmmm, you do that." I watched him closely

He dialed someone on the phone. "Kay, come for a second, please," he told who I assumed to be Kayla.

Seconds later, she walked into the office.

"Take all of these and file them. Make sure to send out the invoices; they're completed," he instructed.

"Kayla, I have something for you to do too." I bit down on my bottom lip, flirting. I got a slight smirk from her, but Chadd didn't like that.

"Kayla, now!" he raised his voice, causing her to grab the files and fly out the office.

I just chuckled at how I was able to ruffle his feathers easily. Noticing a picture of him and Lyric, I decided to fuck with him some more. "Is that your wife you're with in that picture?" I pointed at the photograph I was referring to.

"Yes, it is," he answered while doing something on his computer.

"But, why you don't have any updated photos of y'all in here? She's a bit bigger now, correct?"

He stopped typing and looked up at me with a surprise expression on his face. "How do you even know that?" he quizzed.

"Nigga, do you know my last name?" I laughed. "You should really appreciate your woman more often cause if you don't, a real nigga gon' slide and grab her. You gon' be sick," I teased.

"I'll worry about my wife, thank you."

"Yeah, you do that. But, most of all, make sure you worry about that bread." I looked at the bags that were still on the ground.

I stood up, shot him a menacing glare and turned to leave. There was nothing else to say; he knew what he had to do, and he better had done it right.

CHADD

Being around any of the mobsters made my skin crawl. It was like I was already in my casket in the dirt and the bugs were crawling and eating away at my skin. They were the type of people that it didn't matter if you did wrong to them or not, if they suspected it, that's what they went on.

For a while, the business relationship between Don Luchi and I changed a bit. In the beginning, I wasn't so fearful but, as time went on, I wasn't so comfortable. I felt if I was to die by the hands of them when it was all said and done, why not get something out of it?

While I cleaned their money and made sure everything looked legit, I overcharged for my services from the original agreement. When involved in business relationships as such, it was going to end in either two ways: being killed by them or being arrested for helping them.

When I first got in bed with the Luchianos, I didn't think everything through. I was fresh out of college, just signed to the top investor company and was green to everything. After getting to know the business and doing my proper research on the family and what they had me doing, I knew then and there I had to look out for myself.

"Who were they?" Kayla asked as she made her way back into my office when Logan left.

"Some people that's not to be fucked with," I simply said and continued to wrap up the account I was working on before I was rudely interrupted.

That's one thing I hated about them; they'd just pop up at any time unannounced and expect me to be at their beck and call.

Kayla stood there just staring at me and at the bags on the floor.

"What?" I spoke up and asked.

"What's in the bags?" she went on to pry.

"None of your concern, Kayla."

"Wow, okay, it's like that now? When did you ever start holding stuff from me?" She rested both hands on her hips.

She was right. If it was one person that knew all my business and personal situations, it was her. Kayla knew more shit than Lyric did, and that was my wife.

"Close the door," I said lowly.

I just hope this don't come back to bite me in the ass for telling her, I thought.

She sat down right across from me in the same chair Logan was just in.

"I've been cleaning money for a mafia family for years now," I came right out and said.

Kayla looked at me with a blank stare. "Who knows about this?" she finally spoke up and asked.

"Just you, now."

"Fuck, Chadd. Do you know what kind of shit you're into?" She shook her head in frustration.

Although I was hesitant to tell her the truth, it felt as if I had a weight lifted off my shoulders. Holding that in for all those years with no one to vent to was hard.

"I know, I know," I said softly.

"Don't fuck with these people money." She pointed at me.

"Listen, I'm doing them a favor. Just know I'm taking care of everything and making sure to get mine at the same time," I expressed.

"What the fuck is that supposed to mean?" she asked in a hushed tone.

"Don't worry about it. The less you know, the better," I advised.

"Whatever, Chadd." She waved me off.

"So, you don't want that beach house no more?" I eyed her.

It was like I had two wives because every second, Kayla wanted something and, to keep her happy and her mouth closed, she got whatever she desired.

"Of course, I do, but I don't need anything coming back on you, me or even Lyric," she voiced.

"Now you care about Lyric?"

"You know what, Chadd, fuck you." She stood up to leave, but I got up from my chair and ran to her before she could touch the doorknob.

"I'm sorry, I'm sorry," I plead as I reached over to lock the door. I grabbed her around her waist and placed my lips in the crook of her neck. Blowing gentle air, I started to plant soft kisses to her smooth skin.

"No, stop," she tried to squirm out of my grasp but was unsuccessful.

Holding her around her waist with one hand, I used the other to make my way up her pencil skirt and to my favorite place.

"Mmm, baby, no," she moaned quietly.

"Shhh," I said in her ear.

I unbuckled my belt, undid my slacks, and let it fall to the ground as I hiked up her skirt. She stopped protesting, which I knew would've happened once I felt her get wet. Kayla was always scared when we fucked in the office. Of course, it wasn't allowed, but she was more so worried about what people would say about her messing around with a married man. She never flirted or did anything out the ordinary while at work. As far as everyone knew, we were just on business; I was her boss, and she was my assistant.

I guided her back to my desk, so we had something to hold onto and not make noise against the office door. "Bend over," I whispered in her ear and watched her do as she was told.

I slid my rock-hard dick right in her as I covered her mouth to muffle her moans and cries. Starting out at a steady pace, I picked up my speed, moving in and out of her hole. When I bent her all the way over on my desk, I spread her cheeks and saw the pink of her pussy as I entered and pulled out. I wasn't able to see the beautiful sight of Lyric's pussy like that anymore. To spread her cheeks were a task by itself, far less to see what was going on down there.

I kept at Kayla for a good while until I heard a knock on the door. Instead of stopping and asking who it was, I chose to ignore it. Nobody was going to mess up my nut, not when it was so close; I would've been walking around with blue balls.

The person at the door stood there for a while which annoyed me, but I tried my best to ignore them and reach my peak. Moments later, I carelessly exploded my nut inside of Kayla but, at that time, I didn't care; the shit felt great.

I'll just get her a Plan B, I thought.

I had wipes in my desk, so we wiped ourselves off and quickly got dressed. "Don't leave just yet, wait a while," I instructed her.

The person was knocking not too long ago, so who was to say they weren't nearby. After several minutes, Kayla left. I waited some more time before stepping out and walking around. No one seemed to have any suspicion, so we seemed to be in the clear.

I returned to my office after playing things off and got

right down to work, counting the money and handling the investment.

AFTER SPENDING the entire day counting, I didn't even get the chance to properly place the investment into the account. I told myself I would do it when I got home. I was tired from the counting, which literally took up my whole time at the office, allowing me to do nothing else but that.

By the time I got home, it was already past nine. I was surprised Lyric didn't call or text me since I was supposed to be off hours before. I didn't want to complain about it neither. The less stress I had, the better.

When I entered the house, it was dark and quiet, which led me to think Lyric was already asleep. I kicked off my work shoes, dropped my briefcase off in my office and made my way upstairs.

As my left foot touched the last stairs, I heard soft moans. At first, it took me aback because I didn't remember the last time I heard Lyric moan. Any other guy would've automatically thought their wife was being fucked in their house, but I knew better; she wasn't getting no action.

Creeping through the hall, I quietly approached our bedroom. The door was cracked just enough for me to peer through. Lyric was lying there with the covers over her lower body and her top part exposed. Her breasts had gotten huge, which was the one thing on her body I loved.

She had her head tilted back and she played with and

brought pleasure to herself. I couldn't lie; the sight of her enjoying the orgasm and her breasts turned me on, but something in me just couldn't walk through the bedroom door and give her what she so badly wanted: me and my dick.

I turned on my heels to head downstairs to my office, to leave her at it. When I got in, I noticed my dick was semi-hard, which I knew would've happened after feeling a way watching her. Since I was somewhat in the mood, I closed and locked my office door and did what I usually would, call Kayla.

After dialing her the first time, she didn't answer, so I continued to try calling her but to no avail; she wasn't reachable. I texted her because it was so weird of her not to answer me.

Me: What you doing that you can't answer me? Anyway, my dick is hard, and I need one off, call me when you see this

After some minutes of no response, I chalked it up as she was already asleep. I allowed some time to pass for Lyric to finish and get herself together before I went back upstairs.

When I got in the room, she was fast asleep, so I quietly moved around, got in the shower, and climbed into bed, letting my tired and restless state to take over; I was in a deep slumber not too long after I closed my eyes.

KAYLA

"Ooow!" I screamed out. "Right there, baby!"

I was finally screaming for real that time, not faking anything but sincerely enjoying all the dick I was receiving from Kevin.

"You like that?" Kevin asked as he drilled his way in and out of me from the back.

I swung my head back towards him and shot him a lustful look. "Yes, daddy," I cooed.

He grabbed ahold of my hair and rammed his way into me harder and deeper. Although my kitty was hurting, it felt so good.

"I'm about to cum," he stated.

Perfect, because I am too, I thought.

We both released at the same time, and it felt fuckin' great, like top tier.

I hated when I had sex with Chadd. He would think he was doing something but, in the end, only he was satisfied while I was still sexually frustrated.

"That shit was wet," Kevin joked but, at the same time, I took as a compliment.

"Mmmhmm, yeah, I know," I boasted as I got up from the bed and headed to the bathroom.

Kevin was my off and on boyfriend of five years. We'd known each other since we were kids and eventually started liking on one another. Kevin was fully aware of what I had going on with Chadd. He agreed to not intervene if he was taken care of in the process.

We all got what we wanted. Chadd wanted someone young and sexy as company and to fuck, while Kevin and I got money out of it. My salary that I was paid was cool, but fuckin' the boss was a whole other check.

When I noticed Chadd checking me out and it went from that to flirting, I knew I had gotten a come up. He was head over heels for me and it only got worse, more like an obsession and was willing to do any and everything I asked of him. Once, I asked him to leave Lyric. He was completely for it, but said it had to be done in a smart way because if he was caught cheating or Lyric got a whiff of why he left, she could've possibly end up with everything, leaving him with nothing.

As he gave me money, I would break Kevin off, stash some, and enjoy the rest. Chadd wasn't giving no small-time money. He was giving me large amounts; I'm talking racks. After finding out the revelation of him cleaning money for a mob, now I knew where he was getting all that cash from because although his job paid very well, he was on some millionaire status. So, after meeting the guy in the office that day, it all made plenty of sense how he could afford to spoil both Lyric and I and still have a boatload of money.

"How are things with you and your snow rabbit?" I heard Kevin ask, referring to Chadd.

"Things are good, they're great actually," I answered confidently.

They were. Everything was falling into place and, while Chadd felt like he could trust me, which was true to a certain extent, I had one up on him and got another piece of insurance. He wouldn't have wanted his wife or anyone at that to find out he was having an affair and was heavily involved with a mob.

"I hear you, just don't be over doing it Kayla. I'll break your neck and his," Kevin threatened.

"Baby, relax, I know what I'm doing." I stood by the room door and gave him puppy dog eyes.

"You better. I don't be feeling the fact I have to share you when you're my bitch."

"I know, I know. I don't like the fact I have to be involved with him like that either, but it won't be for too long. It's only temporary," I assured him.

He nodded his head and began texting someone on his phone.

I knew, deep down, Kevin was uncomfortable with the arrangement, but he couldn't really have too much say since I was bringing in bread and his little snatch and go licks wasn't hitting. Someone had to be the bread winner and, at that time, it was me He was dripped in the latest designer and was driving around in a new Kia Cerato, thanks to me and Chadd.

Of course, Chadd was completely unaware of Kevin and who he was to me. I never mentioned having a boyfriend from the moment I met both Lyric and him. If Chadd called me and Kevin was around, Kevin wouldn't say a word or, most times, he would exit the room because he didn't want to hear our conversation. I tried my best to keep the two separate, as in when I was with one, I didn't speak to the other.

Snapping out of my head, I jumped in the shower to wash the sex off. I literally had two men in one day, which sometimes happened more often than I wanted it to. There were times Chadd and I had sex and he left me unsatisfied, so I would make sure Kevin made up for it. While there were other times Chadd did better than usual, which was giving amazing head and, when I got home, Kevin would want sex and I couldn't tell him no because it would've been a whole fight.

Finishing rinsing my skin, it hit me that I had to go and get a Plan B. Earlier that day, Chadd had came in me, something that happened once in a blue moon. I could've counted on one hand the times it happened. I wasn't ready for no children. Kevin wouldn't have let it happen, and it just would've been an overall poor decision. Having Chadd's baby would make us all lose everything; Lyric could've drained him dry.

As I got out the shower, Kevin was on his way in.

"Baby, I'm running to Rite Aid. I have to pick up a few things that I forgot on my way in," I informed him.

"Aight, cool. Be careful and call me if anything." He kissed me on my cheek and proceeded into the bathroom.

I quickly got dressed, throwing on a sweatsuit, Ugg boots, and my Moncler jacket. I was out the door and in the car within minutes. The faster I got to Rite Aid was the quicker I returned home.

Looking on the dash, I saw it was pushing ten o'clock. We lived in a safe neighborhood, so I wasn't worried about anything happening. I just wanted to get back in the warm and out the cold.

Heading to the store not too far away from my place, I pulled into the parking lot and found a parking spot near the entrance. I hurriedly turned off the car, got out and locked it, making my way inside.

I went straight for the aisle that had the Plan B in it but, as usual, it was locked away and I needed a worker to open it. I looked around to see if there was anyone working the aisles but there wasn't, so I made my way back to the front of the store to ask for assistance.

"Hi, can I have someone help me get a Plan B?" I asked the woman behind the register who was cashing out an older woman.

"No, problem, give me one second." She smiled and continued to finish up with her customer.

The older woman who she was helping turned and looked me up and down with a hint of disgust on her face, so I rolled my eyes back at her.

"If you're not ready for a child, just keep your legs closed," she spat, grabbed her bags from the counter, the receipt from the worker and stormed out the store.

"What the fuck was her problem?" I asked out loud.

Both the worker and I bussed out laughing because older women really had a problem. I guess she may have been one of those that were against abortion and contraceptives. Either way, it wasn't my problem. I lived for me, not anyone else.

The employee left from around the register once the lady was gone and another co-worker of hers returned to the front. We walked to where the Plan B was; she quickly unlocked it and grabbed one out.

"Is one fine?" she asked as she handed it to me.

"Yeah, thank you," I answered.

I walked off and headed to pick up some other things off the shelves to show I had to make the sudden store run. If Kevin knew Chadd came in me, things could've turned left with the quickness. While I kept Kevin in the loop of mostly everything, there were certain things that I kept to myself and would take to my grave.

After grabbing a bunch of bullshit, I rounded the corner and ran headfirst into someone. Shaking myself off and picking the items off the ground, I looked up to see it was Lyric and, out of all things she helped me pick up, she held onto the Plan B, looked at it and eventually handed it over to me.

Shit.

"Hi, Kayla." She smiled faintly.

"Hey, Lyric, how are you?" I asked.

"I'm fine, it's been a while since I saw you. How's everything?" She looked me up and down.

"I've been well, can't complain." I shrugged.

She looked at the Plan B in my hands again and smirked.

"You should think about all the women that's having a hard time to conceive before taking that. Maybe it'll be a blessing you get pregnant." She smiled and walked off suddenly.

After she made that statement, I knew she couldn't have known Chadd and I had a thing or else she would've made an opposing comment to the one she made.

I rushed to the register and cashed out my items, made my way to my car, got in and sped out the parking lot. My conscience started to get the best of me, and I started feeling emotional. Lyric was nothing but a nice person from the moment we met. She saw the struggle I had at my job working as a waitress and offered her help to get me out of it and into a better situation.

In the beginning, it was strictly business. I never looked at Chadd any kind of way. He was not only married, but he was white and not my type. But as time went on, more bills accumulated. Kevin wasn't bringing in as much money; everything fell on me. Once I saw Chadd had an interest in me, I took it as an opportunity to get what I wanted with no regard to anyone else but myself.

I wouldn't lie and say I didn't think about Lyric and what we were doing to her, but I realized I had to look out for me because no one else would. It was the kind of life we lived, survival of the fittest, and I was going to make sure I stayed on top.

CHAPTER 12

LYRIC

I woke up after only being asleep for a little while, I saw Chadd had gotten home and made it to bed. Out of nowhere, I had a crazy craving for some ice cream and other snacks. When I went downstairs into the kitchen, it was nothing in there. Trying to ignore the urge, it became unbearable, so I got dressed and went to the twenty-four-hour Rite Aid that was on the Boulevard some ways away from us. What I didn't expect was to run into Kayla and have a Plan B box dropped at my feet.

When I saw the box, I swallowed the lump that formed in my throat. It told me two things; he was fucking her raw and he came in her if she had to get that pill. While I was relieved that she didn't want to have a baby by him, I was also hurt to know they were very comfortable with each other that they were going skin to skin. In my head, I was thankful Chadd and I weren't sexually active; then, I would've been rushing to get tested.

Trying to mask my pain and play things off, I kept it cute and simple. Once I said what I said to her, I walked off to get my snacks. By the time I went to ring up my things, she was gone, which I didn't expect anything else.

I knew guilt came over her once she saw me face to face and, of course, her knowing I saw the Plan B and gave her some bullshit words of encouragement. If I had said anything slick, she would've known I had an idea about her and Chadd.

Picking up my bag of treats, I headed for my car and made my way back home. When I arrived back at the house, I got undressed and back into my night clothes. Curling up on the living room couch, I turned on the TV to find something to watch and started to nibble at my snacks.

A guy who reminded me of Lo appeared on the TV, and I immediately started to think about him. He hadn't written me back, but I knew he must've been trying to handle what-ever with his girl. I told myself I'd reach back out the following morning since I was already late.

I continued to eat and watch TV until I was full and tired all over again. Putting everything up and tuning off the tele-vision, I climbed the stairs and got into bed, falling asleep as soon as my head hit the pillow.

WHEN I POPPED my eyes open, I rolled over and, of course, Chadd was already gone. I reached for my phone on the nightstand and saw I had messages from a couple of people: my mother, Nick, Lori and, surprisingly, Lo.

It was like he was in my head last night because I made a mental note to contact him but, instead, he'd already took it upon himself, which I wasn't mad at.

Lo: Good morning, shorty, everything good with you? I meant to hit you back from your last message, but things been hectic on my end

Me: Good morning, it's fine, I know how life can be. And yes, everything is good over here

I texted him and everyone else back, then went into the bathroom to brush my teeth and wash my face. By the time I was finished making my coffee and cracking my laptop open, another text from Lo came in.

Lo: So, what plan you had on trying to pay me back? Even though it's not necessary

Me: I guess we can go out for drinks and grab something to eat, nothing crazy. I just want to show you my appreciation, that's all

Lo: Oh, so like a date?

Me: No, not a date, I'm married, remember?

Lo: I hear you, but yeah we can do that, when?

Me: Up to you, I'm always free in the evening once I complete my writing goal.

Lo: Lets go out tonight then

Me: Cool, let me know if you want to go somewhere specific, if not I'll find somewhere

Lo: Aight, bet. I'll hit you a little later, I'm finna handle some shit

Me: Okay, cool

I didn't know why I felt deeply wrong for simply having a conversation with the opposite sex, even though it wasn't like that. It didn't help that we had plans to go out for a meal and drinks either, but why should I have deprived myself from having a friend when my husband had a whole other bitch?

Just when I was about to place my phone on *do not disturb* so I could start writing, an email came through. When I opened it, it was the camera footage of Kayla getting out the Uber and running into the house. There was a short message that came with the video.

Hi Mrs. Larson, I'm sorry I took a while to send the video. I hadn't been home to my grandmother's in a while but, when I did get there, she told me to send you this. Sorry for the delay again. Have a great day.

As if it was perfect timing, after feeling a little guilty about my plans, the feelings went right out the window when I saw the video and was reminded that I had done nothing wrong in my marriage. If anything, the video gave me the push to go out and enjoy the company of a new friend, if I could've even called him that.

After I saved the video and tucked the email into my important folder, I finally placed my phone on *do not disturb* and got to work. Although I felt it was a lot going on in my life at the moment, one thing I made sure of was I got my work done because with or without a man, I needed to be able to provide for myself. Plus, writing was my therapy. It was my escape from reality, and I needed it more than ever.

Some hours later, with minimal breaks, I was seven thousand words into my writing goal of only five thousand. When I looked at the time, it was around five o'clock. I was so in tune with my story and it was flowing like a waterfall; I didn't notice so much time had passed without me stopping. When I had tunnel vision like that, it was the best thing for me. I usually exceeded my day's expectation.

Since I completed my major task for the day, I turned my phone off *do not disturb* and checked for unread messages, missed calls and social media notifications. The only one that stood out to me was a text from Lo.

Lo: Eve Ultra Lounge, 8 p.m.

Oh, I guess you did have somewhere in mind, I thought to myself.

Me: Okay, see you there

I looked at the time and saw I had about two hours or so to get ready. Almost immediately, I rushed to my closet to pick out something to wear. As I was browsing, I bypassed a lot of my old clothes that couldn't fit me anymore, which took me down memory lane of when I had all the cutest fits and drew the attention of everyone.

Continuing my search, I made a note to myself to go shop for some new threads because I barely had anything to wear. I barely went out, only having to go to my publisher's office for meetings, run little errands and lunch dates here and there with Nick and Lori. Most times, I was stuck in the house wrecking my brain to come up with a dope ass book.

I came across a cute, long graphic t-shirt. Grabbing that out the closet, I went to find a pair of jeans to go with it. Next, I skimmed through my footwear to see what would've been most appropriate for the occasion.

Once he told me where we were going, I looked up the lounge and saw it was a casual place, so I didn't need to over dress. With that in mind, my eyes landed on these cute ass high heel boots that I knew I had the perfect matching bag to go with it. Just because I gained some pounds didn't mean a bitch couldn't walk in some inches.

I laid out my outfit on the bed and hopped in the shower. Not wasting much time, I handled my hygiene and got right out. Before getting dressed, I applied light make-up to my face and straightened the weave I had sewed in my hair. Once my top look was done and flawless, I proceeded to get dressed.

Just as I was putting on my boots, I heard the front door open and close and the alarm being disarmed, letting me know Chadd was home. Not caring if he was home or not, I continued to put my boots on. Once everything I needed was in my purse, I grabbed it and my phone and made my way downstairs. It was just about time for me to leave out to go meet Lo.

Chadd didn't make his way upstairs. The only place I knew I could've found him was in his office, so that's where I went.

"Hey," I stood by the door and greeted him.

His face was down in his phone so, instead of responding

to me like a human being, he waved at me without saying a word or even looking my way.

"Alright, then, I'll see you later." I turned to leave but was quickly halted.

"Wait, where you going?" he finally spoke up and asked.

When I turned back around to face him, the expression he wore was priceless. He was completely shocked and amazed.

"I'm going out with a friend for dinner," I informed him confidently.

I battled with telling him the truth or lying to him and saying I was going out with Nick or Lori, but I felt I wasn't doing anything wrong so, if he asked further questions about which friend, I would've answered him truthfully.

"Oh, okay. You look nice," he said with skepticism as he sized me up and down.

Wow, a compliment?

"Thank you." I smiled gracefully. "Don't work too hard, see you later." I waved goodbye and walked away from his office to the front door and out the house.

Before I left out the house, I started the car so it would start to heat up. It was dead smack in the middle of winter and the cold wasn't no joke, especially at night. When I was comfortable in the driver seat, my phone's ringtone started to blur through my car's speaker; it was Nick facetiming me.

"Heyyy," I sang when I answered the Facetime call.

"Hol' uppp, where you going, boo?" he asked all excited with a big ass smile on his face.

"Out to eat with a friend," I informed with a grin on my face.

"You look the fuck good." He snapped his fingers.

I took a look at the little box that showed me on my camera, and I sure enough did. It had been a while since I was dolled up and got dressed to go out. I almost had felt like my old self again. "Thank you my love." I blew Nick a kiss through the phone.

"Well, you go and enjoy your night, girl. I was just calling to check up on you and, apparently, you're doing just fine." He shot me a wink.

"I'll call you tomorrow," I told him.

"Promise?" He held up his pinky finger.

Since high school, we always did that corny shit, but it was our own little way of holding each other accountable and keeping our word.

"I promise." I held up my pinky finger as well. "Love you, baby."

"Love you, bye." He blew me a kiss before hanging up.

By the time the call was finished, the car was completely warm inside and out, so I put the lounge address into the GPS and started it. It was about a half an hour away from me, so I backed out the driveway and got on the road to get there on time.

Feeling myself, which felt just a little foreign to me, I bumped some City Girls, Megan Thee Stallion, and Cardi B on my way there. Besides Nick and me knowing I looked good, those songs I played had me feeling like I was Beyoncé out that bitch.

With all the singing along and twerking in my seat while driving, I didn't even notice I was quickly approaching the lounge. I quickly paused the music and called Lo.

"Yo," he answered all nonchalant.

"Hey, where are you?" I asked.

"I'm like two minutes away, where you at?"

"I'm down the block, about to pull up," I informed him.

"Aight, park up. I'll see you in a second," he said and hung up.

Moments later, I pulled into the parking lot of the lounge and found a spot to park in. I waited patiently for Lo to call or text, letting me know he was here or for me to even see he had arrived, that was if he was driving the Porsche Cayenne. While waiting, I got a text from Chadd.

Chadd: I'm going out with the guys tonight, just letting you know if you get home before I do, and you don't see me

Me: Okay cool, be safe, I love you

Chadd: Love you

Looking up from my phone for a quick second, I saw Lo's car pulling up at the front of the lounge. He parked directly in front, shut off his car and stepped outside. That was my que to exit my ride.

Grabbing my purse and phone, I cut my engine and climbed out the car, making sure to take my time planting my heels onto the ground. I saw Lo standing out front looking around for me. As I got closer to him, butterflies started to flutter in my stomach, which was weird. Ignoring it, I strutted my way to him with a boost of confidence.

Once our eyes locked, I instantly became nervous. Lo looked like something I wouldn't have mind bending over for. His whole aura screamed sex appeal and bad boy and, at that point, I wouldn't mind indulging in forbidden acts.

Once in front of him, I eyed his fit, which he was dressed in designer from head to toe. He even had a thick ass diamond-filled Cuban around his neck and wrist with a Richard Mille.

"There you go shorty," Lo said once we were face to face.

I simply smiled because I didn't know how to respond. The only thing I knew how to do was pray. I prayed I had self-control because the man that stood before me was definitely a test.

LOGAN

When Lyric walked up on me, she was almost unrecognizable. Not that she was a totally different person, but her whole appearance and demeanor was different from the other times we were together. I could tell her self-esteem had been boosted, from what and who, I wasn't sure, but she definitely walked with much more confidence than she did before, and I was low-key happy for her.

"Let's get in here and see what's good." I motioned for her to walk in front of me, as we entered the lounge.

I visited the lounge once before and the food was tasteful as fuck; it was clean and out the way. Having any of Cat's friends randomly seeing me out wasn't something I needed again. Things were still rough between her and I, but I hoped it would get better soon. I hated beefing with my wife and having to keep my head focused on the game.

Once we stepped inside, I told the hostess my name and we were led to the section table I had reserved. It was a calm area, away from the people who seemed to be overly enjoying themselves. The tall white couches were soft to sit on, and the tables were just high enough for drinks, food, and hookahs to be placed on. I was impressed just like last time, but I just hoped the food was just as great as before because in a heartbeat, I didn't mind telling a muthafucker to take the shit back.

"You smoke?" I randomly asked her.

"No, I used to back in the days, but the most I'd do now is some Hookah," she giggled.

"I get it, you want to order some?" I offered.

"Yeah, that's cool. Let's get one, but no bullshit flavors." She raised her brow up at me.

"Man, you must think I'm some wack ass nigga or something."

"Nah, not at all."

We both started to laugh.

The DJ was playing all the latest songs making the atmosphere feel like a nice vibe. The volume wasn't too loud. We were able to talk at a moderate level and still heard each other.

While we both looked over the menu, I checked her out some more. She really stepped out for the night. I wasn't sure if this was her all the time when she went out or was it for me. Either way, I was sure she felt she had to look good for the occasion. I wasn't into big bitches, not saying anything was wrong with them, but Lyric definitely made them hoes look good.

"You know what you're getting yet?" she came out and asked me.

"I believe so, but let me ask you first. I don't want to order from a part of the menu and you be like aht, aht, that's how y'all girls be, right?" I joked.

She playfully pushed me in my arm and said, "Boy, shut up. Get whatever you want, I got it," she reassured.

Oh, shit now, let me find out she got the bag, I said to myself.

I leaned back in my seat, smirked, and just waited for the waitress to come and take our orders. Not long after, she did just that. Both Lyric and I ordered food, drinks and agreed on watermelon flavored hookah.

While waiting for our meals, they brought out our drinks and hookah, of course. We just vibed to the music and didn't say much to each other; thankfully though, it wasn't awkward.

"So, who's the joint that popped up on you the other day?" she came out of nowhere and asked, catching me by surprise.

I contemplated about telling the truth or lying. I quickly reminded myself this wasn't real, no matter how real it felt. I was on a job basically.

"Some shorty I been fooling around with for some time; she's very entitled," I chuckled.

"I can see that," she said and joined me in laughing.

I was happy she didn't push with any more questions; she left that topic alone once I answered her. Under any other circumstances, I would've never denied or had lied about my wife but, in that case, I had to play it safe.

"Here you all go." The server came and placed our meals in front of us.

"Thank you," we both said in a unison.

"So, your husband know you out here on a date?" I asked, trying to ruffle her feathers.

She took a forkful of mash potatoes, swallowed and shot me a look. "Now, you know this ain't no date, just two friends hanging out," she corrected.

"Friends? Oh, okay, we're friends now. That's cool, I guess."

"Let's just hope your chick don't pop up here starting no mess because I don't have time." She eyed me closely.

You and I both.

"Nah, I doubt it. Besides, like you said, two friends out enjoying each other's company."

"Right," she giggled. "You wouldn't be interested in me anyway," she added and continued to laugh.

Off rip, she was saying the truth, and it's not because she's on the bigger side, but because she was totally the opposite of me. She was quiet but also had a mouth on her when necessary. She didn't go out; she was a homebody, which any man should be appreciative of. If it wasn't for my pops putting me on her, our paths would have never crossed and that was a fact. We lived two different lives.

"What makes you say that and what makes you so sure of your statement?" I took a sip of my drink and waited for her response.

I could tell my reaction and questions took her aback because instead of answering right away, she paused like she was thinking of an answer.

"Lo, please, look at me and look at you. I mean, I look good and you look good, but our looks are just two different looks, if you get what I'm saying," she expressed.

True.

"Elaborate," I told her.

She took a sip from her glass and took a deep breath in and out. "Okay, I'm not sure what kind of lifestyle you live, but you seem to be in the streets, I'm not there. I saw your chick and, based off of that, I can see your type, which isn't me," she pointed out.

"Hmmm, I hear you, shorty. What if I told you, I ain't have a type and I went off chemistry and shit?" I tossed her a curveball to throw her off.

"Then, I'd say I apologize for the judgement made," she simply said.

"Apology accepted." I shot her a smirk, which made her blush uncontrollably.

Got her, I thought.

"You definitely different, Lyric, and different is most times a good thing."

"Thanks." She continued to blush. "I guess I can say the same," she stated, staring at me in my eyes.

After a few moments of a stare-down, she finally pulled

her eyes away from mine. We continued to eat, drink, and make conversation. I could tell she was becoming more and more comfortable around me, which was what I needed. I couldn't front though; Lyric was a cool ass chick. It was refreshing to be around someone different and who wasn't trying to get something out of me.

The lounge was closing, but we were still having a good time. When I checked my phone, it was only ten forty-two p.m.

"You done for the night or you tryna go hit up a club?" I asked her.

She thought for a moment; then, a smiled graced her face. "Fuck it, let's go," she giggled.

I called the waitress over to get the check and, when I started to pull out my wallet, Lyric tapped my hand and shook her said no. She went into her purse, got her wallet, and pulled out her card, handing it over to the woman.

It felt weird as fuck allowing a woman to pay for my shit, but I knew I had to play along. At least the waitress saw I attempted to pay but was stopped by her, so I didn't look crazy or nothing. Think about it. What a nigga like me, dripped in the latest fashion and have crazy jewelry on, looked like letting a woman pay for our night?

"I got the club," I stated sternly. She lifted her hands up in surrender and smiled.

Once the waitress returned with her card and had her sign, we grabbed our belongings and got up out of there. I made sure to walk her to her car since it was in the parking lot and it was late. Seeing she was secured and ready to follow me, I hopped in my vee and pulled out, leading the way to a spot that was usually jumping on that particular night.

We drove a little way but got there in a quick enough timeframe since it was late and barely any cars were on the road. I shot Lyric a quick text telling her to stay behind me where I pulled up and valet her car.

Getting out our vehicles, she walked up and met me, as I eased my way past the line and to the entrance.

"Big Lo, what's good my guy?" one of the regular bouncers greeted me.

I dapped him up, along with the two other guards that was out front with him. When Lyric got right behind me and I signaled that she was with me, they let us in without any issues. I told the girls at the booth I wanted a section and, without hesitation, they quickly scrambled and led us to a roped-off VIP section that had the perfect view of the entire club.

I loved being able to see everything and everyone around me. It was a must to be able to scan the room and see what was lurking or coming my way. "What you drinking?" I bent down and asked Lyric in her ear.

"Anything, just keep it light," she suggested.

We were already drinking Casamigo and Patron at the lounge, so it was only right we continued drinking that. I waved over a bottle girl and told her what to bring. I slipped her the money for the bottles and a few extra bills for her services. The look shorty gave me when she saw her tip, she smirked at a nigga and looked like she was ready to do other things.

Not long after, she and two other girls returned with the bottles, bucket full of ice, chasers, and glasses.

"Is there anything else I can do for you?" the same bottle girl I tipped asked.

"Nah, I'm cool, ma. Good lookin'," I told her. I returned my attention back to Lyric and started to make her a drink.

"How the hell we gon' drink all this?" she yelled above the music.

"We're not." I smiled at her.

It was an unspoken rule. No matter the occasion, even if it's a quick pop up, if you're a nigga with paper, you had to order a minimum of five bottles. In instances like that, I'd just give the unopened bottles away to ladies on the dance floor on my way out the club. That shit didn't put a dent in my pocket; it didn't even measure up to snack money.

Once both of our drinks were made, we made a silent toast and enjoyed the rest of the night.

About an hour and a half later of a good vibe, I saw Lyric froze up and was staring in the direction of the bar. Following her gaze, I saw she was looking at none other than her weak ass husband, Chadd, and his side bitch, Kayla. Of course, I knew who they were, but she didn't know I knew so, quickly changing my demeanor, I started to act confused.

"You aight, shorty?" I leaned into her ear and asked her.

She continued to stare at them with so much hurt in her eyes; I felt it as if it was me.

Damn man. I shook my head.

She unlocked her phone and went to the camera. After she took a couple of snaps of the two, she locked her phone back and placed it in her purse.

"Who's that?" I asked, even though I already knew the answer.

She looked at me with watery eyes. "Can we leave?'" she asked.

I nodded my head up and down. She grabbed her bag and started to walk out the VIP section before I even lifted a foot to leave. Following behind her, I noticed she kept her eyes trained on Chadd and Kayla. I was wondering if she was going to approach them or not but, once I saw she was getting near to the exit, I knew she was taking the high road.

Once outside the club, I handed the valet boys our tickets, so they could bring our cars around. The whole time we waited, Lyric was quiet and spaced out. I wasn't sure how to approach her; I didn't do well with situations like that.

When our vehicles both pulled up, I walked her to hers. As she was getting in, I pretended to pry once more. "I saw you eyeing a couple in there. Who were they?" I pushed.

She took one last look at me, and I saw a tear drop down her cheek.

"My husband," she simply answered in the saddest tone ever.

She got in her car and closed the door. As I took a few steps back, she drove off without even saying goodbye.

Although I had no deep connection with her situation, I still had a heart and I felt her pain. No woman should ever witness their husband out with another woman, enjoying themselves at that.

Cat and I had our history, but one thing I never did was disrespect her publicly. All my broads were seen behind closed doors, and they were fully aware of my marriage. What Chadd was doing was beyond fucked up and I could've only imagined how he treated her at home.

Dickhead.

LYRIC

Hearing conversations or even reading them of your husband cheating was one thing, but actually witnessing it with your own two eyes was a whole other ball game. The night I saw Chadd and Kayla together at the club all booed up fucked with my mental something serious. I couldn't breathe, even when my heart was beating uncontrollably.

The man I loved, the man I trusted, the man I placed my whole life into his hands and vowed to do right by betrayed me in the worst way. Although I knew they were fooling around, it didn't quite process until I actually saw them together.

Days had passed since that night. Lo had been reaching out to me, but I kept it short with him because I wasn't in the right head space. I felt so embarrassed that the one time I was out with a friend for the first time, he saw what I saw, and it didn't make any sense that I lied about it. He would've later found out. Even though I wasn't speaking much, Lo continued to send encouraging words and checked up on me. I was appreciative of him since he was the only one who knew what was seen that night.

While going through a depressive stage, I had to continue to play dumb, so I locked myself in the guestroom whenever Chadd was home, which was a limited time. I told him I had caught the flu and a bug and didn't want him to get sick. Whenever I heard him come in, I would simply go into the guestroom with my things or already be there, knowing it was time for bed. It worked out perfectly for me, and I prayed it did because I wasn't ready to face him knowing what I knew. Damn near a week had passed and I kept up that act. He was so full of himself and into Kayla, he didn't even push to see if I was dying or if I was fine.

On a Thursday morning, there was a knock on the bedroom door, which woke me up from my slumber.

"Lyric!" Chadd yelled from the other side of the door.

"Hmmm?" I groaned loud enough for him to hear.

"I'm leaving for a convention trip for the weekend. I'll be back on Sunday," he blurted out.

I didn't even have the energy to question him or even get upset; it was passed that. "Okay, I hope you have a great trip. Be safe," I responded.

"Let me know if I have to send someone over to tend to you. I hope you get better by the time I get back."

"I'll be fine, go ahead."

"I love you," he mentioned before walking away from the door.

"I love you, too," I said above a whisper.

We were tossing around the L word like it was a meaningful thing between us when it wasn't. I basically cringed when he said those words. What I didn't understand was how he thought it was okay to randomly tell me he was flying out to a convention last minute like I was his little girlfriend or something. Chadd did things with no regard to my feelings or even had enough brains to make me at least feel important.

Giving him enough time to leave out the house, I rolled out the bed and made my way to the window. Peeking through the curtains, I saw him putting his luggage and stuff in the car.

Oh, this mutha fucker had this planned, I thought as I nodded my head up and down slowly.

When I saw him pull out the driveway, I went and unlocked the bedroom door, finally able to roam the house freely without having to avoid him. Although I was able to breathe a little, I felt drained and empty inside. I needed to release what all was on my mind, so I went for my phone and went to the group chat with Nick, Lori-Ann, and me.

Me: SOS, I need y'all like right this minute, please!

Not wasting a second, everyone responded right away.

Nick: I'll reschedule my client, I'm on my way

Lori: Calling the sitter now!

They knew it had to be something urgent and that it couldn't wait if I told them to come now. Even when something was important, I would try to water it down and sugarcoat it, so openly telling them something was wrong was a red flag to them.

I knew it would've been a good hour or two before they both got to the house since Nick lived in the city and Lori in Brooklyn. They both drove, so I knew it was only a matter of wrapping up what they were doing and getting through traffic.

While waiting for the pair, I jumped in the shower, brushed my teeth, and made myself look presentable. I didn't remember the amount of times I even bathed my skin in the past week while I kept myself locked up in the room and away from Chadd. I barely ate, so far less for handling my hygiene.

Finally looking at emails and text from everyone else that I had missed for those days, I saw Irene was trying her hardest to reach me, text, calls, and emails. After reading over her emails, it seemed my release date and party for my book was set. While I should've been excited for it, I couldn't care less at that moment. There were more pressing things in my life. I made a note for myself to reach out to her when I felt up to it.

As usual, there was a morning text from Lo.

Lo: Good morning, beautiful. I hope you're feeling better than yesterday. Remember, no matter how bad the

feeling is, it's temporary. I hope you have a great day, shorty.

For a second, I was just about to lock my phone, but I decided not to be rude. Lo had been checking in on me from the moment shit hit the fan, so I texted him back.

Me: Good morning, thank you for all of the uplifting messages. I appreciate you checking in on me, means a lot.

Once I hit send, I went and curled up on the couch, turned on the TV and waited for Nick and Lori to arrive. Not long after I found a calm show to watch, I heard my doorbell ring. Getting off the couch, I went to answer the door thinking it was Nick or Lori, but I was hit with a surprise instead; it was a delivery man holding a bouquet of roses.

The first thing that came to mind was Chadd left knowing he went to be on some bullshit, so he tried to sweeten me up while I was stuck home getting cheated on.

"Good morning, ma'am. I have a delivery for a Miss Lyric," he announced.

"Morning, that's me," I plainly said.

"Here you are." He handed me over the roses and swiftly walked back to his truck.

I stood in my doorway confused and annoyed all at the same time. While I was getting ready to go back inside and close the door, I heard a car beep its horn. Looking around the roses, I saw it was Nick and Lori both pulling up at the same time. They pulled into the driveway and quickly hopped out their cars, making their way to me.

"Lyriccc!" Nick sang as he did a light jog to me with Lori

following behind him. "Ooowww, what's this?" He grabbed the bouquet of roses and smelled them.

"I still don't know, honestly." I shrugged.

Nick stared at me for a moment, then grabbed me in his embrace for a big hug. "My poor baby," he cooed.

When he let me go, Lori immediately ran in and hugged me tightly.

"Thank you guys for coming," I spoke, as we all made our way into the house.

Everyone kicked off their shoes and jumped on the couch in the living room. Not wanting to waste time, Nick started rattling off question after question.

"So, what's up? Everything good with you and Chadd? Is he here? Do I have to fuck him up?" Nick went on.

"Damn Nick," Lori snapped on him.

We all started laughing, something I hadn't done in days.

"Give me a second and I will tell y'all everything, okay?"

I put my hand up to motion for them to give me time to think. I was trying to figure out where to start. From our last lunch, I informed them of the whole phone call situation but, like we all agreed, I needed to get some solid proof and that I had plenty of.

"Before I start, let me do something real quick," I told them.

Nick and Lori stared at me with suspicious looks. I called Chadd's office and placed it on speaker for them to hear.

"Good morning, Walter and Green Incorporated, how may I direct your call?" the receptionist answered.

"Hi, good morning, can you please put me through to Mr. Larson, please?" I requested.

"I'm sorry, but Mr. Larson is on vacation right now. May I take a message?"

"Oh, no, thank you. You can just put me on to his assistant, Kayla."

"I'm sorry, ma'am, but she's on vacation as well," the woman added.

Nick and Lori-Ann had blank expressions on their faces as they continued to listen.

"Oh, okay. Thank you so much then. I'll try back at a later date," I quickly said and hung up.

I had a mind that he wasn't going to no funky ass convention because he would've been talking about it for a while before it was even time for him to go to it. It was the perfect excuse for him to get away for a few days where I wouldn't bother him because I'd think he was working. Little did Chadd know, I was smarter than I even led on, but he should've known that he didn't marry no dummy.

"Tea, now!" Nick demanded sternly.

"So, I told y'all that I had a mind Chadd and Kayla were fuckin' around, right?" I asked.

They both nodded their heads up and down.

"Well, Mrs. Lawrence across the street caught on her camera Kayla coming out of an Uber and running into the house and staying here for hours the very same day I heard their call, which was when I had the meeting and had lunch with y'all."

I showed them the video on my phone, then took a deep

breath before I continued, "He's been having a lot of late nights and, when I called Kayla, she would cover for him saying he's at dinner meetings. One night, about two weeks ago, I ran into her at Rite Aid late at night; homegirl was buying a Plan B." I curled up my lip.

Both Nick and Lori gasped but, before they could say a word, I put my finger up to stop them. I wanted to finish; I wanted to lay everything out on the table before they started with any questions or comments.

"Last weekend, I went out with a friend." I stopped and looked at Nick because he was who I spoke to before I headed out. "While out, Chadd texted me and told me he was going out with the guys, but it was a lie. I saw him and Kayla at the same club I ended up going to after dinner."

"Get the fuck out of here!" Nick jumped up and shouted.

"Wait, did they see you?" Lori asked right away.

"No, I was in a section, and they were at the bar. I did get some good pictures of them though." I showed them the photos I captured.

"Wow, this shit is wild as fuck," Nick expressed.

It truly was. It was some shit straight out of a Lifetime movie, except I didn't have plans on killing them, but I was going to kill Chadd's pockets.

"I'm so sorry, Lyric," my sister spoke solemnly.

"Me too, baby," Nick chimed in as he made his way over to hug me. "No wonder you've been distant these past couple of days. You were giving us one-word answers or weren't answering at all. Whole time I thought you were just busy writing and got caught up, not knowing you were going through this shit all by yourself," Nick went on.

"I need a drink; I don't even care what time it is," Lori suggested.

"I second that," I laughed.

The situation wasn't funny, but I had to laugh to relieve some pain and heartache. I honestly felt better once I told Nick and Lori everything, I needed to know I wasn't bugging out and I was for real going through that situation.

Nick stood up and was on his way to the kitchen but stopped and grabbed the card that was poking out of the roses. "Who's Lo?" he came out and asked.

The roses are from Lo?

Now, that was a twist I didn't see coming. The whole time I thought Chadd had sent them because who else in the world would just randomly send me anything?

"Remember the friend I told you I went out with? Well, it's Lo," I confessed.

"Hmph, well, okay, bitch, tell us more," Nick stated excitedly as he took his seat again.

I ran down the story of how we met and how each of our interactions went. Due to the fact I never had a picture of Lo or had him on any social media, I had to describe to them how he looked and, of course, Nick didn't believe me with his extra ass.

"Well, this friend sounds like a good thing," Lori spoke up and said.

"I agree, mmmhmmm," Nick agreed.

"We're just cool y'all," I laughed at the two of them. They just knew how to drag shit.

"If I were you, honey, I would see what this friend is about. If he willing to sling some slang, I would happily take it, no strings attached. Y'all just friends, right?" Nick tried to persuade me.

Once he mentioned that, he had my brain turning like working wheels. Lo was fine as fuck and, by the way he carried himself, I knew he had a big dick. Chadd was my husband and all, but I'd had better before him. And since he hadn't touched me in almost a year, what Nick was suggesting wasn't such a bad idea. I mean, I was being blatantly cheated on.

"Nick, you're a hot ass mess." I wagged my finger at him.

He shot me a sinister grin and winked.

"On a serious note, what are you going to do?" Lori-Ann asked.

"It's time to see a lawyer."

CHAPTER 15

LOGAN

I knew Lyric was taking shit hard. Not that the situations were the same, but I had a similar experience with Cat, which led to our marriage becoming fucked up. The difference was I didn't think Lyric was the cheating type and, as far as I read up on her, she was always loyal to Chadd. If she ever stepped out, she did it well because we knew nothing about it, but it was highly doubted.

The way she would respond to my messages, it was like she barely wanted to even speak, but I understood. I knew I had a job to do, but I also felt for her and her heartbreak, that was the part I didn't sign up for to witness.

Against my better judgement, I ordered a bouquet of roses and sent it over to her. Knowing Chadd's schedule, by the time the delivery got there, he'd been gone. Even if he wasn't, I didn't give two shits. One, he wouldn't have known exactly who it was from and, two, he probably needed to see his wife was getting attention elsewhere; it would've sparked jealousy in him.

When I got the text from Lyric with the rose emoji, I knew she'd received it. I hoped that it made her feel a little better and special at the same time; that was sincere from the heart.

"Mr. Luchiano, you have a visitor," Luci stated from behind my bedroom door, pulling me from my thoughts.

I grabbed my phone and looked at the time; it was only seven in the morning. "Who is it?" I questioned because I was confused as to who the fuck had the nerve to be pulling up to my crib that hour in the morning.

"It's your father," she informed me.

Cat jumped out of her sleep as she heard who it was and looked at me. If no one put fear in her heart, it was my pops.

The old man is back. I laughed.

"Aight, I'll be down shortly," I told her. "Get yo ass up." I gave Cat a stern look.

I slid out of bed and went straight into the bathroom to brush my teeth and wash my face. Going into my walk-in closet, I changed out of my pajama pants and threw on a Nike Tech sweatsuit, slid my feet in some Nike slides and left out the room.

As soon as I reached the staircase, I looked down and saw four of my father's guards standing by the front door to my house, two on the inside and two on the outside. The Don was always heavily guarded. I think he had more security than the president.

Descending the stairs, I rounded the corner and saw my old man sitting comfortably on one of the sofas in the living area.

"Good morning, son." He smiled.

"Morning, papa, why you ain't tell me you were back?" I kissed him on his forehead.

"Surprise," he beamed with his arms open wide.

I shook my head and just laughed; my father was something else. "Come on, old man, let's go in here." I motioned for him to follow me into my man cave.

Once we were in the room and the door closed, we got right down to business.

"What's the update on the wife?" my pops inquired.

"I'm not sure if she knew before, but she finally saw ol' boy out with his side joint at the club when we went out. Shorty hurting bad," I informed him.

"Oh, you two went out?" He raised his eyebrows.

"Yeah, out to eat, then the club," I confirmed.

"Nice, so how was the visit to the office?"

"He was shook. I could tell he's full of fear, but that don't mean shit when money is involved."

"True, very true," he agreed and spaced out for a moment. "The accountants are almost finished with the audit, so we'll know sooner than later."

"Bet, what you need me to do until then?"

"Keep getting closer to her, take the goods if she gives it."

"Papa, you want me to fuck this girl?" I stood up from my seat.

He shot me a mean grill, making me return to my seat. "I need her to trust you all the way so, if and when I decide to make my move, it will be easy," he explained.

"Aight, yo," I gave in, not like I had any other choice.

He got up from his seat at the bar and made his way to the door. "How's Cat?" he asked.

"Cat is Cat," I answered.

"Hmmm, women," he chuckled as he walked out the door.

A few seconds later, I got up and left out the room as well, walking right into Cat and my pops having a little reunion. I watched the two have their exchange; they finally ended it, both looking my way.

Cat had a history of trying to kiss my father's ass, so she would run and tell him about every little thing like a little ass girl. And my pops, he used that to his advantage at times.

"Call me, Logan," he said before exiting the front door.

I nodded my head in acknowledgement and proceeded back into my den.

It's always something extra with him, man, I thought.

I sat back and started thinking about different things to get into with Lyric, like what places she would go and what she'd enjoy. I scrolled through Instagram and found myself on Google, bussing my brain on ideas. Then, it clicked.

She was an author, so she had to be into any kind of literary events. I searched up some book expos and I was just in luck; one was happening the very next day. The only thing left to do was persuade her to come with me, which I knew was a possible fifty, fifty chance with her mental state. All a nigga could've done was tried, so I did.

Me: You can talk?

Surprisingly, she texted right back.

Lyric: Yeah

I pressed the call button next to her contact and let the phone ring.

"Hello?" she answered in a low tone.

Part of me was feeling a kind of way. I was basically preying on her while she was going through a tough ass time.

"Wassup, shorty? What you dealing with?" I asked.

"Nothing, just laying here watching TV. What you up to?"

"Relaxing myself, soon make a move. I hope yo ass ain't been depressed in the bed over that wack ass nigga," I blurted out.

The phone went silent; I didn't even hear her breathing.

"I'll be aight," she finally spoke up and said, then let out a long, loud sigh.

"Nah, this shit ain't right, ma. Fuck that, we're going out tomorrow," I suggested but more so demanded.

"Lo, where you trying to go?" She let out a light laugh, giving a good sign that the conversation was going in the right direction.

"I'm not sure, but just be dressed and ready for around noon," I told her.

Sighing loudly again, she cleared her throat before speaking.

"Fine, just don't take me anywhere else that I'll potentially run into my husband and his hoe," she joked but was serious.

"I got you, don't even worry about that."

"Alright then. Oh yeah, how did you know my address to send those roses? Thank you again, by the way."

"I hollered at my folks at the shop. Your address was in your registration file when you took the car there, and you're welcome," I explained. I made that lie up from the moment I sent the roses; I knew she'd ask.

"Ohhh, makes sense," she giggled.

"Yeah, crazy but listen. I'll hit your line a little later; I have to go handle some shit."

"Okay, be good," she told me.

"Always."

"Yeah, okay. Bye, Lo," she laughed and hung the phone up.

I looked at my phone and laughed. Low-key, I was happy I was able to put a smile on her face. Since my plan was going smooth, I got up and headed back outside to let Luci know to fix me something to eat. I opened the door to my den and Cat was in the motion of walking away from the door.

"You being a creep again?" I asked, stopping her in her tracks.

"What are you talking about, Logan?" She tried to act surprise.

"Bro, you wasn't just listening by the door. What I told you about that weird shit?" I barked.

"I wasn't even b—"

"Man, whatever." I waved her off. "Aye, Luci! A nigga

hungry around here!" I yelled as I walked in the direction of the kitchen.

I was over Cat and her stalkish ways. What she needed to do was be more of a wife and things would be at peace under our roof. Ignoring her, I went and found Luci, so I could fill my stomach and start my day.

CHAPTER 16

LYRIC

Nick and Lori-Ann ended up spending the entire day with me, which I needed. I was so grateful for them and how they dropped everything to be by my side. Instead of speaking on the situation, we joked and made future plans that had nothing to do with the bull-shit I was going through. For a minute, I forgot all about my problems but was quickly reminded when they left, and I was in the house alone.

Once they left, I tucked myself into bed and went right to sleep, hoping the following day brought some kind of joy, which it did in a way. Lo reached out and asked me to go out with him. I wasn't sure where we were going, but any place other than the house was better. So, taking Nick's crazy advice, I was going to entertain my little friendship I had with Lo.

The day had come for my outing with Lo. Keeping up the appearance from the last time we went out together, I pulled out a nice fit from my closet. While I got dressed, there were a few times I had doubts of falling through with my plans.

Flashes of conversations with Chadd making fun of me rushed my brain. If he saw me that way, why didn't Lo? I had so many questions for Chadd, Lo, and even myself, but Nick's voice made its way into my head.

"Everyone isn't the same. Don't allow one sorry ass fuck to make you write off all men," he advised.

Shaking off the negative feeling, I turned on some hot girl music and started to dance my way around the room as I got ready.

"Easy (easy), does it (does it). These bitches ain't bussing shit, these bitches, busted (busted). You know this box is like my watch, this shit, flooded (flooded)," Megan Thee Stallion rapped on her hit song *Budget* featuring Latto.

I rapped along as I applied my make-up to my pretty plump face. Once that was done, I stepped into the jeans I was going to wear and jumped a couple of times to get them up, then lied down on the bed to pull them up even more. I moved my hips as I squeezed the last bit of my beautiful thighs into the jeans.

I put my shirt on and threw my long Fendi sweater over my body. Looking at myself in the mirror, I liked what I saw. To complete my outfit, I chose to go with a pair of black Givenchy boots since I wasn't sure where we were going. I knew it couldn't have been anywhere I had to dress all fancy; it was during the day, and he would've told me.

Pulling out the hair pins I had in my hair to hold up my curls, I allowed them to flow down since I was all the way ready to go. The last thing I had to do before leaving out the house was dumping all my things from my other bag into the one I was using that day. As I was doing so, my phone started to ring. While I thought it was Lo, I looked and saw it was Irene.

Shit, I forgot to hit her back, I cursed myself.

"Hey, Irene," I answered, trying to sound normal as possible.

"I mean, I thought you were dead or something. Where have you been?" she jumped on my case right away.

"I'm sorry, I've just been dealing with some things. I apologize."

"A simple text goes a long way, Lyric. Anyway, I was reaching out to let you know the release is on for next week so, whatever you have going on, make sure it doesn't get in the way of it," she demanded.

"No problem, it won't," I assured her.

I had no plans on allowing what was going on to get in the way of my success. I worked hard on the book that was about to release, so there was no way I'd let Chadd's trifling ass knock me totally off my square. He distracted me for damn near an entire week, but I promised myself I'd make up for it.

"Alright, I gotta go, we'll talk later," she said before disconnecting the call.

Dropping the last bit of things in my bag, I looked myself in the mirror once more to make sure I looked right. I left out the room and headed downstairs, finally making my way out the house to go meet Lo.

———

AFTER DRIVING to the address he sent me, which was in New Jersey, I pulled up to the Prudential Center. Immediately, I thought we were attending a basketball game or something, so I was happy with the outfit I picked to wear.

While calling him to see where he was, I circled the surrounding blocks to look for a parking spot.

"Where you at, shorty?" he asked as soon as he answered the phone.

"I'm like two blocks away from the address, looking for a parking spot," I explained.

"Man, if your simple ass don't come to the front of this joint and valet your car," he instructed.

This nigga loves valet parking.

"You must be paying for it," I said sarcastically but was dead ass serious.

"Come on now, I think you should know me better by now."

"Mmmhmmm, I'm coming," I told him and hung up.

I bussed a U-turn and drove back to the front of the center, where I saw him now getting out his car and taking a ticket from the valet boy. I pulled right behind him, slid out my car and did the same.

"Check you out," Lo stated as he looked me up and down with a smirk on his face.

"Nah, check you out, Mr. Drip," I retorted.

Lo was always full of swag, even if he had on something simple as a Nike Tech sweatsuit. His tall, athletic frame was eye catching, making him noticeable as soon as he entered a room or area.

"Man, come on." He smiled.

As we got closer to the entrance, the signs were much clearer, so I was able to see what kind of event we were attending and, if I told someone I wasn't shocked and excited at the same time, I'd be lying. Lo brought me to one of the most popular and biggest book expos in the country.

"Are you serious?" I beamed brighter with every step I took closer to entering the center.

"Dead ass serious," he boasted with a grin.

"I can't believe you," I said above a whisper with my hands covering my mouth but, apparently, he heard me because when I looked up at him, he was smiling ear to ear.

When we got inside, we were greeted and asked to present our tickets. Lo pulled his phone out, let them scan the code, and we were allowed entry.

Stepping foot inside, I was in total awe. The place was filled with people, not too crowded where it was unable to work but just the right amount of heads to make the event a success.

There were authors all over the place, behind their booths and tables selling their books and interacting with readers. I knew off the back I was leaving the Prudential Center broke because I was definitely buying hella books. Before I was a writer, I was an avid reader and, even when I was in the process of writing a book, the urge to turn a page and read was always happening.

"How did you even get tickets?" I quizzed.

Tickets to this event was hard to come by. People been on the waiting list for years and never got through. It was almost like an exclusive thing for top authors and high sadity readers.

"I know some people." He winked at me.

At that point, I didn't give two fucks who the person was; I was very much grateful for the connect.

We walked around the center, stopping at almost every other table to talk meet and talk to authors, as well as buy their books. I made sure to mention that I was an author myself and hoped to be in their shoes one day. Networking was key in the literary industry so, with that being said, I made it my duty to let the readers know about me while on my little journey around the place.

"Who's your favorite author?" Lo came out and asked as we continued to walk around.

"John Grisham and James Patterson," I answered proudly.

"You mean, that John Grisham and James Patterson?" he asked, pointing in front of us at two men standing up talking with readers side by side.

"No, fucking, way," I gasped.

I rushed over like the groupie I was for them and potentially waited for the other readers to finish up. By the time it was my turn, I was speechless when I had them standing right in front of me; Lo was the one that had to speak on my behalf.

The men gave me some solid advice, which inspired me to want to continue perfecting my craft. They were down to earth and, after a few moments, I was finally able to speak, so I told them a bit about myself, and they followed me on Instagram and Twitter. I received free autographed books from them, and they told me I could reach out whenever if I ever needed them. The whole experience was top tier and I had nothing else to compare it to; it was just that great.

Lo and I continued to make our rounds, as we approached a crowd that was standing by an author's table. It seemed as if the person was super popular because it was the most people I saw at one table at once. I wasn't able to see who it was since they crowded all the signs and banners.

Once we were basically by the crowd, the people started to part like the red sea, and that's when I was hit with the ultimate surprise. It was my very own table with my books and other goodies for readers.

"What!" I screamed out in joy. "No, no, no. No freaking way!"

That's when Irene appeared from behind the crowd and fist-bumped Lo.

"You two? But how?" I pointed between Lo and Irene.

However they set everything up and whenever they got the chance to, they were slick as shit because I had not one bit of a clue, but I wasn't even mad.

"I'll explain everything later. You have readers to holler at." Lo motioned for me to engage with the crowd.

I couldn't do anything but smile brightly as I went ahead and did meet and greets with my fans.

LATER THAT NIGHT when I returned home, I was beyond exhausted but still feeling like I was on cloud nine. The day I had was unbelievably amazing, not one part of it wasn't a movie.

In the short period of weeks Lo had been in my life, he'd done something so meaningful that my own husband probably never even thought of doing. I know people say it's the thought that counts, which was true but, from what Irene told me, Lo cashed out some bread for me to even be able to be a part of the expo.

Lo did everything in his power to make sure my spirits were lifted from the hard fall I'd taken. And although he set everything up, he took the back seat and let me enjoy my day without hovering over me; it was like he wasn't even there. But every time I turned and looked for him, he was right there in the cut, smiling, being genuinely happy for me.

I wasn't sure how I was going to repay him, but I knew one thing for sure and two things for certain; if he even gave me the slightest hint he was willing to give up the dick, I was going to jump my big ass right on it and enjoy the ride.

LOGAN

W hat I did for Lyric wasn't fake or a part of the plan; that shit was done from the bottom of my heart. I'd never met someone who was so passionate about their craft as her. Most chicks I came across and attracted just wanted to be kept; they ain't have shit to offer but pussy, mouth, and headaches.

Besides my pops telling me to continue getting close to her, I felt she deserved what I did for her. She needed a major uplift because I knew her world was quickly crumbling beneath her feet. It was also rewarding to help someone shine in a dark time.

With the bullshit her husband was doing, I just prayed he settled shit properly, so Lyric wouldn't get hurt any more than she already had been. Our friendship was something I didn't mind having after all but, if shit was to hit the fan, although it would hurt me, I knew my place and that was with my pops.

The following day after the expo, I woke up to a text from Lyric with her own plans for the day.

Lyric: Good morning Drip God, get up, brush your teeth, and wash your ass, we're going out to brunch

Brunch? What the fuck kind of nigga she think I am?

The only meals I knew were breakfast, lunch, and dinner; all that other fancy shit was nonexistent for me.

Me: If you want to go eat, just say so. Good morning to you too, and let's link for two

Lyric: lol, okay, that's cool

I looked at the time and it read nine seventeen a.m. Still feeling a bit tired, I locked my phone and went right back to sleep for a little while. As soon as I got back comfortable in bed, Cat walked in the bedroom with a tray and placed it right in front of me.

"Good morning, baby," she sang as she lifted the cover over the plate, revealing the food underneath it.

Inhaling the delicious scent and looking at how fine the food looked, I woke up fully almost instantly.

Now this is how a wife supposed to act, it's the simple things, I thought as I looked at her with a smirk.

I wasn't sure what had gotten into her, if she heard the voice in my head the other day about her changing or what but, either way, I wasn't complaining. It was the correct baby steps in the right direction.

"Enjoy your meal." She smiled and left out the room.

And that's exactly what I did.

I HAD JUST FINISHED TYING my laces to my Balenciaga sneakers. I stood to my feet and looked at myself in the mirror, content with how I looked as usual. I grabbed my phone and wallet off my nightstand and left out the room.

As I was descending the stairs, my phone rang loudly. When I looked, it was my father calling.

"Papa," I answered.

"Come see me," he ordered and hung up.

I reached the bottom of the staircase and just took a deep breath in and out before running my hands down my face. It was one thirty in the afternoon and I was supposed to meet Lyric for two o'clock but, of course, when the old man called, I went running.

As I jumped in my Benz truck, switching up my ride for the day, I pulled off my estate and headed straight for my father's. On the way there, I shot Lyric a text that I'd be about a half an hour late. Right as I was pulling through the gates of my father's place, she wrote me back, simply saying okay.

When I stopped and put my truck in park, I cut the engine and exited out the car. As I made my way up the steps, the front door opened with his housekeeper standing there to greet me.

"Good afternoon, Logan," she sweetly stated.

"Afternoon," I politely responded, making my way into the house.

"Son, is that you?" I heard my pops yell out from the kitchen.

I walked further in and rounded the corner to see him sitting at the island counter. "Wassup old man? What's so urgent you needed to see me last minute? I got shit going on," I jumped straight to it.

"Come sit." He nodded his head in the direction of the bar stool next to him.

I pulled my phone out my jeans and rested it on the counter as I took a seat. "What's up?" I asked.

"The accountants finished their audit. Larson been skimming a lot of money from us," he informed me.

Fuck. I really didn't care for the clown ass nigga; it was Lyric I was more so worried about.

"So, what we finna do?" I eyed him closely.

"I'll confront him about it. Hopefully, he admits to it and will be willing to pay back," my pops said with a shrug and took a sip of his coffee.

"You think it'll be that simple?" I raised a brow.

"Hopefully was the key word I used. His wife will be having a release event for her book this week coming. If he doesn't budge when I have a little chat with him, we'll attend the event to remind him how touchable they are."

And this was what I didn't want to happen.

"Say less," I simply said.

If I was that fool, I'd try to make amends anyway possible

with Don Luchiano because things were bound to get very ugly in a short period of time if not.

After my pops and I chopped it up a little more about other affairs and family business, I hurriedly got up out of there and made my way to meet Lyric. I told her to meet me at my uncle's shop, that way she could leave her car there and hop in mine.

By the time I arrived, Lyric was already there and waiting for me. I wasn't too badly off with time, so I hoped she wasn't one of those females to start bitching because a nigga was ten minutes late or something. I climbed out my truck and walked over to her vehicle.

"Nice of you to make it," she said sarcastically with a grin when she rolled down her window.

"My fault, I had to make a quick move. I'm here though, right?" I lifted my hands up.

"Yeah, yeah." She waved me off.

"It's cold as fuck out here. You getting out the car or you staying there?"

She rolled her eyes, put up her window, and turned off her car. By the time I turned around to return to my truck, she was locking her doors and walking behind me.

As soon as she climbed in the truck, I placed it in drive and pulled off.

"I just sent you the address," she told me.

I looked at my phone and clicked the blue highlighted address, directing it to my maps.

"Damn, why all that traffic?" she exclaimed once the route

popped up on the screen in my truck. "By the time we get there, we won't even have reservations."

"Yeah, that traffic going to the city looking kind of crazy, and I don't feel like being in it, no cap," I expressed.

"We can find something else to do on the island," she suggested.

"True, or we can just order food, get some drinks and stay in and chill." I looked over at her to see her response and body language.

"But where? Chadd comes home today, and I don't know your situation at home." She curled her lip up.

"We can go to my place, that ain't a problem," I offered.

The house that Cat and I shared was not the only spot I had. I had two in the city, one in New Jersey, and another one on the island, but she didn't need to know all of that of course.

"Okay, so let's just do that then," she agreed.

I made the next right turn to head back in the opposite direction we were going. As I got near my condo, I pulled into the nearest plaza that had a liquor store and a good tasting Chinese restaurant. Killing two birds with one stone, we hit up both places so, once inside, we didn't have to leave back out until it was time to.

Gathering everything we needed and wanted, I drove over to my condo, getting there fast as hell since it wasn't far from the shopping plaza. We quickly got out the car, grabbed the food and drinks, and rushed inside to beat the cold breeze.

"I pass this building all the time. I always said it looked

classy, neat and clean, but that's an understatement now seeing the inside," Lyric stated as she looked around while we walked to the elevator.

"Yeah, I thought so too when I first saw it; that's why I had to get a spot here," I agreed.

The elevator was already on the first floor when I pressed the knob, so we simply stepped inside. I pressed the floor and allowed it to take us up. Reaching the floor, I allowed her to get off first with slight directions to where the condo was. Walking down the long hall, we finally reached the door. I opened it and let her in as I followed right behind.

Without telling her to, she rested the bags she was holding down on the table that was near the door and slipped out of her boots. She picked the bags up and slowly walked further inside as she took in the scenery.

I didn't spend a whole lot of time at the condo, but it was well put together and made comfortable for me. Anytime I really couldn't stand being home or I had a late night of handling something and felt it wasn't safe to go home due to a possible tail, I would crash there.

"Yeah, I should've known you was gon' be living in some shit by the way you dressed and the whips you push," she smirked at me as she rested the bags down on the kitchen counter.

"Yeah, whatever man, it's aight," I responded while looking around.

We laughed it off and immediately started emptying the bags. I grabbed some plates out of the cabinets and glasses, filling them with ice. She took the food out while I made us some drinks. We made our way into the living room to eat and find something to watch.

"Hmmm, this taste good; they know how to cook," she complimented the food.

"Yeah, they a different kind of Chinese," I laughed.

"I see," she giggled and took another bite of her chicken.

We munched, drank, laughed at some comedy show we found of Kevin Hart, and just kicked back and enjoyed each other's company. I hadn't chilled with a female like that in years. I remembered when Cat and I use to be that way before we were even married, when it was just fun and good vibes.

A few hours later, a number of drinks and unless laughs, we were still Netflix and chilling.

"Yo, his little ass funny as hell," she cracked, referring to Kevin Hart.

"No cap, that nigga is hella funny. And I ain't in the habit of laughing at the next nigga jokes," I chuckled.

"Shut up." She playfully slapped my arm.

We were seated side by side on the couch. She had one of her legs propped up while the other was touching dangling.

"Watch your hands." I raised a brow.

"Or else what?" She shifted in her seat to look at me better.

"If you get to touch me, then I get to touch you." I shifted in my seat to face her.

My statement definitely didn't go over her head because she started blushing.

"Then, touch me then. I won't stop you," she said seductively.

"Man, listen, you don't know what you gon' get yourself into," I tried to warn her.

She leaned over and ran her hands from down my legs up until she reached my dick area. Instead of touching my manhood, she squeezed my thigh and just stared at me.

"Maybe I don't care," she claimed.

Without neither of us saying another word, Lyric slid off the couch and onto the floor but positioned herself between my legs. She tugged at my belt buckle and jeans, finally getting them undone. She reached into my boxer briefs and pulled my semi-hard dick out.

Taking in the size for a few seconds, she finally wrapped her lips around my head, sticking her tongue in my pee hole and causing me to brick up instantly. Lyric made her way down my whole pole, making sure to get it wet. She sucked it so passionately, you would've thought she was in love with my shit, but I knew she would be once I broke her off.

Spitting on my dick, she stroked it with her hand with a good amount of squeeze before returning her mouth to it. She bobbed slowly, then picked up her speed, allowing me to fuck her face. I thrust my hips upwards, making sure to hit the little thing in the back of her throat each time.

After having enough, I gently pushed her off and watched her lick her lips. "Take your clothes off," I demanded.

For a second, she hesitated, and I knew from her experience with her husband she was probably self-conscious, but I was a grown ass man so I knew how to appreciate all different kinds of beauty.

"I rather not," she said softly, still kneeling on the floor.

I sat up and got directly in her face. "I don't give a fuck about not a roll on your body. That shit means nothing but more for me to grip and, the way I'm finna dig you out, you'll be grateful you have something for me to pull on. Strip and let me see that ass, shorty."

Looking at her reaction, it almost seemed as though her eyes got watery a little. But she stood to her feet and started to peel her clothes off one by one until she had just her bra and underwear on.

Lyric was beautiful, and it took a real man to realize that. Her curves enticed me; she had natural thickness that a bunch of bitches went to Dr. Miami to get from their fat. She had the most gorgeous face ever, and her personality took the cake; she was one of a kind.

I had her follow me into the bedroom where I undressed myself along the way. By the time we hit the bed, I was ass naked with my dick at attention. I laid her on her back, started kissing her on her neck while making my way down to her plump breasts. I felt her shake a little, so I went back up to her face and landed a wet kiss to her lips. I think she was surprised but, for a second, she froze. I did it again and, that time, she started to kiss me back with much passion.

Once I bit down on her bottom lip, I positioned my dick at her entry and, without any warning whatsoever, I penetrated her. Lyric was wet as fuck, snug and tight. As I made my way in and out of her, a nigga thought he was gon drown, and the only reason was she was flowing like a mutha fuckin' waterfall.

The way she felt, I knew it had been a while that someone

touched her, which I didn't even mind, being as though I was just a little careless and went in raw. But I had confidence she was clean and untouched by the way she carried herself and from my own research and findings.

With our mental and bodies in synced, we fucked for hours, and it didn't even feel forced. A connection was being built between the two of us and it was out of our control. I just hoped when it was time, I was able to separate my feelings and my loyalty.

LYRIC

"Where the hell you been? I called you as soon as I got home and, now, you're strolling in here at midnight smelling like alcohol," Chadd nagged.

I had to take a second to see who the hell he was talking to. "You talking to me?" I quizzed, squinting my eyes.

"Yes, where you been, Lyric?" he pressed.

"I should be asking you that," I mumbled as I dropped my things on the floor on my side of the bed.

"What's that?"

"Nothing, Chadd, nothing. I was out with a friend, and I had maybe a little more drinks than I should." I shrugged.

"That's very unlike you but okay."

I ignored his comment and went into the bathroom to take a shower. Not really wanting to get Lo's scent off me, I knew I had to; it wasn't something I was able to throw in Chadd's face right at that moment. But once I went and saw a lawyer, which I had plans on doing so the following day, I would've been free to do what the hell I wanted in due time.

After an hour of standing under the water just daydreaming about what went down hours before, I finally stepped out the shower. I wiped the mirror and looked at myself. I almost recognized myself, in a good way. I smiled brightly at my reflection because I felt so great inside. I felt alive, and I didn't want it ever to end.

When I stepped out the bath, Chadd was still up and watching something on the TV, which was so odd. He barely watched television and far less for him to still be up.

"How was the convention?" I asked as I sat at the edge of the bed and applied lotion to my skin.

"It was great, network and met a lot of people, learned some new things," he claimed. "I see you're better from your flu. What did you do while I was gone?" He looked my way.

"Yeah, feeling way better," I said with a grin on my face. He couldn't see because my back was turned to him. "I just got some work done as usual and went out with Nick and Lori," I kept it sweet and short.

"That's good, I'm glad you weren't missing me too much," he joked and let out a light chuckle.

"Trust me, I didn't," I mumbled under my breath.

"Huh?"

"Nothing, was just rapping lyrics to a song." I turned and

smiled at him. "Oh yeah, my release party is Friday," I informed him.

"Oh yeah? I'll make sure to have my schedule cleared and off work early," he volunteered, shocking the hell out of me.

"Awwwhhh, thanks baby," I told him.

I literally cringed inside saying that because I knew I didn't care if he was there or not. But, until things were out in the light, I had to play my part as well as him and continue to portray this happily married couple's image.

My phone vibrated on my nightstand, and I had a mind it was Lo. Not caring one way or another, I picked my phone up and checked it.

Lo: Hope you good baby girl, have a goodnight

Me: I am, thanks. Goodnight handsome

A smile appeared on my face as I pressed sent and, apparently, Chadd noticed.

"Who got you smiling?" he pried.

"Nick, with his crazy ass," I lied.

"Mmmhmmm."

I didn't care what he was thinking because he didn't give a fuck when I felt a certain way when he was texting Kayla on the low while right in front of me. Climbing in bed, I got comfortable under the sheets and, within a few minutes, I was knocked out cold.

THE NEXT MORNING, I woke up feeling refreshed and ready to start my day. I had a clear and positive mind. The main task for the day was to visit a lawyer, return home and punch those keys on my laptop to play catchup with my word count.

I'd been researching divorce lawyers for a while since finding out about Chadd's affair. Doing intense research, I finally decided on someone I wanted to move forward with, so that's who I went to see.

"Mrs. Larson for Mrs. Daniels please," I told the receptionist when I walked into the lawyer's office.

"Yes, she's expecting you, come with me." The young girl stood from behind the desk and walked me down a hall and to an office.

When I walked into the office, I was greeted by a young, slim African American woman; she looked just like her pictures online. I felt it was important to go with a woman because they would fight for another woman more than a man would.

"Hi, Lyric." She extended her hand.

"Hi, Mrs. Daniels." I reached out and shook her hand.

"Please, I like to call my clients by their first names, especially when the last name will soon be no more," she explained as we took our seats.

"I like that, I have no problem with that," I laughed.

She opened a file and started to ask me basic questions, as well as verified my identity. Once we discussed what it was I needed from her, we came to an agreement and finalized our business with a signed and paid retainer.

"Now, let me see the evidence you listed," she stated.

I handed over my phone and allowed her to swipe across

to the different pictures and videos. Trying to be organized, I placed everything in one folder so it was easy to locate.

"Hmmm, oh yeah, we can definitely get everything," she looked up from the phone and said, emphasizing the word everything. "Are you involved with anyone, and would he possibly know by any chance? I need you to be honest with me, so we can be prepared if anything," she explained.

I took a minute to answer because it was a tricky question. For all our marriage, I was faithful, and I felt I still was until the very end. Having sex with Lo, in my mind, I was single. I left Chadd the moment I found out he was cheating, and he obviously left me a long time ago.

"I recently befriended someone and, when I say recent, I mean within weeks, but we only been intimate once and it was yesterday. We've been just friends up until then, so I don't think he knows anything at all," I came cleaned.

"Thanks for being honest." She smiled and wrote down some notes.

We continued to discuss what would take place next and what I should do in the meantime. She said for me to still play things cool, until she officially filed the papers with the court, which was going to happen after her private investigator collected more evidence. Once I saw what he had found, I would sign and the process would continue.

I walked out of Mrs. Daniels' office feeling like my time was finally coming. I would've been free from a man who not only betrayed me but humiliated me and treated me like shit. I would be free to find true love again and live happily.

Knowing things were going to change soon, I continued to

keep my head down and act as normal as possible. The entire week, I did my normal things: write, go grocery shopping, and I sneaked and saw Lo a few times. I attended my release meeting the day before it was supposed to happen, and that was about it. I kept things cool within the house, not wanting to raise any suspicion.

RELEASE DAY HAD ARRIVED AND, from the moment I opened my eyes, it had been a movie. My book was officially released to the public around eight o'clock in the morning, so I was being sent a bunch of congratulations texts and posts on social media.

I jumped out of bed with a burst of energy and excited to start my day. Chadd had already left for work as usual. He claimed he was going to get off early, so he would prepare for the party later that night, but all I could've done was wait and see; it wouldn't have made or break me.

The day before, I made sure to hit up the nail and hair salon, so everything was done. I didn't want to have to run and do shit like that last minute and have potential delays. There was nothing really for me to do until the party, so I made it my duty to be present on social media to promote my new release and answer my readers.

Love and support was thrown my way from every angle. It was overwhelming, and I had to respond to so many people. I was busy engaging all day. Before I knew it, it was time to get ready for the release party.

Both Chadd and I jumped in the shower, me in the room and him in the guest bedroom, so we could be on time. He did indeed keep his world and was home earlier than usual. I was surprised but I didn't allow it to distract me from his true self. I knew the only reason he made it his duty to be by my side for the event was because he didn't want to look like a fucked up, unsupportive husband.

Quickly getting dressed, having my make-up and hair in place, we were walking out the front door right on time. He decided he wanted to drive us to the hall, so I didn't even put up a fight. I was going to allow him to feel like he was doing something to make me happy, I guess.

Being that the hall wasn't far from us, we arrived faster than we expected since there was no evening traffic. Pulling up to the front, there were people lined up to get inside as if it was a damn party at the club. Chadd let me out, went to park the car and hurriedly came back by my side before I walked inside.

Walking in, everyone started to clap and cheer for me. I loved the feeling of being recognized for all my hard work and, by the day's sales report Irene had sent me, my book was doing pretty well.

"Congratulations, baby." Chadd kissed me on my cheek.

"Thank you." I smiled.

"There she is." Irene came with her arms wide open to hug me. "Another hot release!" She hugged and kissed me.

I was floating on cloud nine, so my response to everything and everyone was a bright smile. The place was decorated nicely, my books were propped up and a stack was on a table for when it was time for me to do the signing part of the evening. The event team definitely did their thing.

Making my way around, I greeted and thanked everyone for coming, as well as met some new people. Chadd followed me around like a newborn puppy, and I was his mother. It was kind of annoying, but I tried my best to not show any type of irritation.

"Baby, why don't you invite John or someone to keep you company?" I suggested in a nice manner.

"You cool with that?" He looked surprised.

"Yeah, go ahead. You know I have to talk to people and I have the signing."

He nodded his head and walked off slowly as he got on his phone to make a call. I didn't care who he invited, as long as it wasn't Kayla.

The night went on and everything was going nicely. More people arrived and showed love, including Nick, Lori-Ann, and my mother. That's when I noticed the one person I really wanted to be there, wasn't. I knew it would've been playing with fire if I had invited Lo; plus, he understood why he couldn't attend.

I was missing him so much at a point I thought I heard his voice, until I turned around to see it was him and I wasn't hearing shit.

What the fuck is he doing here?

He was in the corner with a group of men that looked Italian, and one stuck out to me; it was his uncle that I saw the last time at the shop.

"Irene!" I called out to her but not loudly.

She ran over immediately. "What's up? What's wrong?" She looked panicked.

"What is he doing here?" I nodded in the direction of Lo.

She turned around to see who I was talking about and faced me again with a confused expression. "I don't know. I didn't invite him." She shrugged.

Nervousness crept into my system because not only did I not need him or Chadd to cross paths, but being in the same room as him was hard for me when I just wanted to hug and kiss him.

"You fuckin' him, aren't you?" Irene asked, curling up her lip.

I lowered my head and started blushing. "It's new, but I'm getting a divorce. Don't say anything, no one knows yet, not even Chadd. I found out he's cheating," I quickly explained.

"Get out of here," she slowly exclaimed.

I felt eyes looking at me, so I scanned the room and landed on Lo; he was staring a hole into me. We locked eyes and didn't move an inch for a good minute until Irene snapped me out of it.

"Stay in line, your very much still husband is here," she pressed.

"You're right." I shook my head and looked elsewhere.

Searching for Chadd, I saw he was in the corner with John, who eventually came to the function. He kept glancing at me and then at the gentlemen Lo was with. Still with my eyes trained on both set of men, I tried to make a connection but nothing came about.

I walked over to where Chadd was and, immediately, he grabbed me by the arm and pulled me close to him.

"Did any of those men over there say anything to you?" he asked in a worried tone.

"No, why? You know them?" I inquired.

"It's business, don't worry about it," he brushed it off.

Business? Wait, they knew each other?

I was beyond confused and needed answers, but it wasn't the place or the time. Feeling a rush of emotions, I ran outside to the back of the hall to get some air, away from everyone and everything.

"Breathe, Lyric, everything will be fine," I whispered to myself.

"Everything will be fine, shorty," I heard Lo say.

I jumped and turned around to see him standing there.

"What you doing out here in the cold and it's dark?" he asked.

"What are you doing here is the question," I shot back his way.

"My father told me to come along with him to a book release event that he sponsored, so I came, not knowing it was yours," he explained.

Once he told me that, I kind of relaxed because I thought he was here to be petty or something. "Oh, by chance, does your father have any business with my husband?"

"That I can't answer, all I—" He stopped mid-sentence to answer his ringing phone. Holding up one finger, he mouthed, "Give me one second."

A few moments passed as he listened to the person on the

other end of the line. Finally, he hung up but had a regretful expression as if he received bad news. I heard footsteps coming from around the corner, and I prayed like hell it wasn't Chadd coming out to check up on me.

"Lyric, I'm sorry," Lo stated.

I turned back to face him because what in the world was he sorry for?

"Sorry for what?" I asked, all confused.

A hand was wrapped around my stomach while a cloth came over my mouth and, within seconds, my whole vision went blank, Lo being the last person I saw.

TO BE CONTINUED

COMING SOON

ACKNOWLEDGMENTS

It wouldn't be me if I didn't say, thank you. I appreciate y'all for rocking with me always. Without you, there's no me.

-P. Wise

ABOUT THE AUTHOR

P. Wise (Pretti Wise) is an emerging author of fiction literature, whose experiences and imagination have shaped her to write about her ideas. She is originally from Trinidad and Tobago but grew up in Bed-Stuy, Brooklyn; also spent a great deal of time in Philadelphia and Chester.

Having experienced and witnessed different events in her life, she has a variety of perspectives that almost any and everyone can understand. The love to write stemmed from a young age, as she enjoyed essay writing and penning her journal.

Coming from a lower-class family, she's a first-generation college graduate, but also, the first to enter and survive a federal prison sentence. With ambition, intelligence, and absurdly high tenacity, she'll have her place in the fiction game.

P. Wise has a 1 year old daughter, who's her world and reason for her grind.

This is P. Wise's eleventh book since starting her career in January 2022.

STAY CONNECTED

Instagram: @CEO.Pwise

Facebook: Author P. Wise

Facebook Business: Authoress P. Wise

Facebook Group: Words of the Wise (P. Wise Book Group)

ALSO BY P. WISE

A Saint Luv'n A Savage: A Philly Love Story

Luv'n a Philly Boss: A Saint Luv'n a Savage Spin-off

Kwon: Clone of a Savage

Kwon: Clone of a Savage 2

Welcome to Cherrieville: Bitter & Sweet

Summer Luvin' with a NY Baller

Tamia & Tytus: A Toxic Love Affair

Diary of a Brooklyn Girl

Sex, Scams, & Brisks

Sex, Scams, & Brisks 2

Made in United States
Orlando, FL
01 March 2023

30573002R00104